Laurie's locker door was hanging open and Matt was crouched motionless beneath it, his blue eyes flashing a glare that would have disintegrated a Martian. Laurie's books were scattered all around him, while her tennis balls were bouncing merrily off in three different directions.

I could just die! Laurie thought. *Right here and now. I don't deserve to live!*

When she opened her mouth to speak, her voice came out as a cross between Donald Duck and Porky Pig. "M-Matt, I—I'm terribly sorry. I—I thought it was shut tight! Are you okay?"

Matt did not say one word. Very slowly and deliberately he unfolded to his full six feet and stormed off down the hall.

Laurie gazed after him in stunned silence. *I must be the biggest airhead in the history of Western civilization,* she thought dismally.

Bantam Sweet Dreams romances
Ask your bookseller for the books you have missed

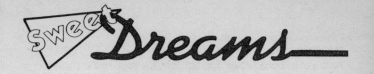

FINDERS KEEPERS

Jan Washburn

BANTAM BOOKS
NEW YORK • TORONTO • LONDON • SYDNEY • AUCKLAND

RL 6, age 11 and up

FINDERS KEEPERS
A Bantam Book / April 1994

*Sweet Dreams and its associated logo are registered
trademarks of Bantam Books, a division of Bantam
Doubleday Dell Publishing Group, Inc. Registered in U.S.
Patent and Trademark Office and elsewhere.*

Cover photo by Kim Hanson.

ISBN 0-553-56478-1

Published simultaneously in the United States and Canada

*Bantam Books are published by Bantam Books, a division
of Bantam Doubleday Dell Publishing Group, Inc. Its trademark, consisting of the words "Bantam Books" and the por-
trayal of a rooster, is Registered in U.S. Patent and
Trademark Office and in other countries. Marca Registrada.
Bantam Books, 1540 Broadway, New York, New York
10036.*

PRINTED IN THE UNITED STATES OF AMERICA

OPM   0 9 8 7 6 5 4 3 2 1

To the great young people of Project Serve

Chapter One

Laurie Adams battled her way down the crowded corridor, clutching her textbooks in front of her like a shield. It seemed as though the whole student body of Chilton High had organized a giant pep rally in the hallway. Dodging elbows, Laurie was trying not to listen to her best friend, but in spite of the babble of voices and the metallic clang of locker doors, Jane Gardner's voice came through loud and clear.

"Laurie, tell me you don't mean it. You're kidding, right? I know you're going to try out for the musical!"

Although Laurie could pretend not to have

heard, how could she pretend that Jane wasn't hanging on to her arm? Taking a deep breath, she turned to look at her friend just as an oversized football-player type shouldered his way between them, breaking Jane's grip and sweeping her into the crowd as though she were an opposing linebacker.

Don't give in, Laurie insisted to herself. *You're not trying out for* My Fair Lady. But she couldn't erase the images that kept flickering through her mind—opening night, the costumes, the bright lights, the scenery, the music. . . .

"It's not too late to change your mind," wheedled a small voice inside her head. "They'll be holding auditions all afternoon, and tomorrow, too."

Laurie slowed to a stop next to the big double doors that led to the auditorium. She felt the stage drawing her like a magnet—and then someone stepped heavily on her foot.

"Hey!" an indignant voice complained. "If you're going to halt in the middle of traffic, how about giving a hand signal or something?"

"Sorry," Laurie mumbled. As she began walking again, she could feel her cheeks reddening to match her sweater.

But the spell was broken, and she let the curtain fall on her daydreams of stardom. *You are not going to change your mind,* she told herself firmly. *For once in your life, you are going to do something right!*

The crowd was beginning to thin out a little, and Laurie heaved a sigh of relief as she made her way to her locker. *How could just three textbooks weigh a hundred pounds?* she wondered, putting the books down on the floor. After she took her jacket out of the bottom locker, Laurie prepared for her daily struggle with the stubborn combination padlock on the upper one. It was in the top row, and she had to stretch to her full five feet seven inches to see the numbers on the dial. She was still fiddling with the combination when Jane appeared at her side, looking frazzled.

"I swear I'm going to get myself a helmet and some shoulder pads!" Jane complained.

The picture of dainty little Jane in football gear was so ridiculous that Laurie had to laugh. "Great idea," she said. "Maybe you can go to college on an athletic scholarship!"

Laurie tackled her lock again, but Jane had reached the end of her patience. "Laurie

Adams, stop that!" she ordered. "Forget the dumb lock and tell me what's going on. You *can't not* try out for the show! You'd be a perfect Eliza Doolittle—everybody says so."

Squaring her shoulders, Laurie faced her friend. "Jane, I'm not trying out, and that's all there is to it."

"But you've got the best voice in the whole school. There's nobody else who can sing that part," Jane wailed. "We'll have to give Ms. O'Connor CPR when she finds out you're not auditioning!"

Laurie felt her resolve beginning to waver again. Ever since Ms. O'Connor had announced that the music department in collaboration with the drama club was going to present *My Fair Lady* for their spring production, Laurie had been picturing herself in the role of the flower seller from the London streets. She had practiced a cockney accent on her family until her brother Tom had threatened to buy her a one-way ticket to England, and she already knew all the songs and most of the dialogue. In all modesty, Laurie felt that Jane was probably right. Nobody else could play the part as well as she.

"But *why*?" Jane persisted.

4

"Because I have to get a job," Laurie told her, turning back to the lock.

"A job? But why now? Why can't you wait until after the show? Couldn't you . . ." Jane's voice faded away.

Surprised by Jane's sudden silence, Laurie glanced down at her just as the padlock finally opened in her hand. Jane sidled closer to her and said in a stage whisper, "Laurie, Matt Harding has been standing over there for at least five minutes, and he doesn't look happy. I think he wants to get to his locker."

Laurie felt her throat go dry and her hands grow moist. Matt Harding was the best-looking guy in school, but he was about as friendly as a block of ice. Unfortunately, Matt's locker was directly under Laurie's, and now he was leaning against the wall on the other side of the hall, scowling at her, his arms folded across his chest as though he were trying to restrain himself from doing permanent damage to someone. *Probably me*, Laurie thought nervously.

Hoping her vocal cords still worked, she said, "Oh, hi, Matt! I—I didn't realize I was holding you up. I'll be out of your way in a second."

Hastily, Laurie shoved her books into the

crowded locker and slammed the metal door. "Let's go," she said, grabbing Jane's arm and nearly yanking her off her feet.

They had taken barely three steps when Laurie heard the crash. It sounded as though the entire library had just dropped through the ceiling. She stopped in her tracks, afraid to look back as she pictured the scene behind her—something along the lines of a plane crash or a train wreck. It was only when she looked down and saw she was still holding the padlock in her hand that she realized what had happened. *I forgot to lock the door!* she thought in horror. *Space Cadet strikes again!*

Very slowly Laurie and Jane turned around. As Laurie had anticipated, her locker door was hanging open. Matt was crouched motionless beneath it, his blue eyes flashing a glare that would have disintegrated a Martian. Laurie's books were scattered all around him, while her tennis balls were bouncing merrily off in three different directions. Pages from a loose-leaf notebook fluttered to the floor like autumn leaves, and her book report lay balanced precariously on one of Matt's broad shoulders.

I could just die! Laurie thought. *Right here and now. I don't deserve to live!*

When she opened her mouth to speak, her voice came out as a cross between Donald Duck and Porky Pig. "M-Matt, I—I'm terribly sorry. I—I thought it was shut tight! Are you okay?"

Matt did not say one word. Very slowly and deliberately he unfolded to his full six feet, brushed the book report off his shoulder, stepped over *World History* and *Algebra II*, and stormed off down the hall.

Laurie gazed after him in stunned silence. *I must be the biggest airhead in the history of Western civilization,* she thought dismally. "Oh, Jane," she sighed as Matt disappeared around a corner, "he was *so* mad! How could I have been so stupid?"

Jane didn't reply. With her hand clamped over her mouth, she was trying to smother her hysterical laughter and could only shake her head helplessly.

Unable to see the least bit of humor in the situation, Laurie began cleaning up the mess. Grimly she gathered her books while Jane scampered off to round up the tennis balls. After Laurie had stacked her books neatly and tucked the balls into the farthest corner of her locker, she closed the door very carefully, fastened the padlock, spun the combination, and tested it twice. This time it was definitely locked; there was no doubt about it.

Jane was still shaking her head as they headed for the exit. "Matt will probably never speak to you again as long as he lives," she giggled.

Tugging up the zipper on her jacket, Laurie tried to pretend that the subject of Matt Harding was of no interest whatsoever. "He hardly ever talks to anyone anyway, so I guess it's no big deal."

"He's so handsome he doesn't *have* to say anything." Jane rolled her eyes in appreciation. "I bet Elaine Desmond would do a handstand on the flagpole if it would get Matt's attention."

Laurie refused to admit, even to her best friend, that Matt's blond good looks had the same effect on her. In her favorite daydream, Matt suddenly thawed out and discovered that she existed. But the dream definitely didn't include burying him under an avalanche of books, and Laurie decided that she might as well forget Matt Harding.

Pushing open the front door of the school, she said, "Come on—let's hit the road."

Jane hung back. "So you're really not going to the audition?"

"Jane, for the last time, I am really not going to the audition," Laurie said with a sigh as she started down the steps. "I'm going home to look at the classified ads in the paper, and I'm going to find a job."

"But, Laurie, there *aren't* any jobs in Chilton," Jane said, hurrying to catch up. "We couldn't even get hired at Burger Castle or Food Circus last summer, remember? When someone has a job in this town, they don't quit until they're ready to retire, or die!"

Laurie tried to ignore her friend's prophecies of gloom and doom, but as they skidded along the icy sidewalks, she knew Jane was right. Chilton, Massachusetts, was not a big city, and jobs, particularly jobs for teenagers, were scarce. Still, Laurie refused even to consider defeat.

"I just have to go on Operation Save," she said, half to herself, "and that means I have to get a job."

"Operation Save?" Jane echoed. "Is that

one of your aunt Melissa's crazy work projects in South America?"

"It's not crazy," Laurie said patiently. "It's really great. And it isn't in South America, either. It's on St. David, a little island in the Caribbean. Aunt Missy always takes some seniors from her school on her expeditions, and I've been begging her for years to take me, too. This year she finally decided that I'm old enough to go, even though I'm only a junior. The other kids are already raising money to pay for the trip."

"What's Operation Save all about?" Jane asked. "I mean, what's it supposed to accomplish?"

Laurie felt her enthusiasm bubbling up. "Well, we'll be on St. David for two months this summer. There was a terrible hurricane last fall that destroyed half the buildings on the island, so we're going to mix cement and lay bricks to rebuild the schoolhouse."

Jane groaned. "Laurie Adams, I don't *believe* this! You actually want to work yourself to death for months raising money so you can go to some grubby island and work yourself to death for two *more* months?"

Grinning, Laurie said, "Oh, I imagine I'll live through it. I'm tougher than I look."

"How much money do you have to make?" Jane asked.

"Well"—Laurie swallowed hard—"just nine hundred ninety-five dollars. That will pay for everything—the registration fee, round-trip airfare, and room and board on St. David."

"Nine hundred ninety-five dollars!" Jane gasped. "It'll take you forever to earn that kind of money!"

"I'm sure I can get donations for most of it," Laurie said, sounding far more confident than she felt. "My dad said his Rotary Club would chip in, and I know my church will help. But Aunt Missy says I have to earn the two-hundred-dollar registration fee myself to prove that I'm really serious about the project."

"But if you're not going down there until summer, why can't you earn the money after the show is over?"

Laurie's show of confidence wobbled slightly. "Because the registration money has to be in by March thirtieth."

Jane stared at her. "You have to come up

with two hundred dollars in *three weeks*? That's impossible! Can't you just ask your parents for the money?"

"No way," Laurie said, shaking her head. "It costs a fortune to keep my brother in college. I even hate to ask Mom and Dad for lunch money."

"But what if you give up the chance to be in *My Fair Lady* to look for a job and then you don't *find* a job?" Jane asked reasonably enough. "You'll have missed out on everything."

"I'm going to find a job," Laurie insisted, "and I'm going to find one today. Going on Operation Save is much more important to me than some silly musical."

But as she marched bravely ahead, she wished that Eliza Doolittle would stop dancing the tango inside her head and singing, " 'The rain in Spain stays mainly in the plain . . .' "

If only she didn't have to choose between the play and Operation Save! But Laurie knew she couldn't have it both ways. Today was March ninth, and time was running out.

They crossed Main Street, jumping over the ridge of snow that lined the curb. *New England winters are endless*, Laurie thought, and sang under her breath, "The snow in Mass. stays mainly on the grass!" She tried to focus her thoughts on the balmy breezes and tropical foliage of St. David and was mentally relaxing from her labors under a coconut palm when they reached her house.

Bending down, Laurie picked up the evening paper from the front steps. "Want to come in and help me check out the classified ads?" she suggested.

"I guess, but I still think this is a crazy idea," Jane grumbled. "Every time you start out trying to help somebody, you wind up in a mess yourself."

"I do not!" Laurie said indignantly, digging in her pocket for the front door key.

"Oh, yeah?" Jane scoffed. "What about the time you donated your father's good raincoat to the church rummage sale?"

Laurie blushed. "Well, it only cost five dollars to buy it back, and it *was* for a good cause."

"And how about the time we collected all those glass bottles for a crafts project at the nursing home, and the bag split open right in the middle of Main Street?"

"Oh, that!" Laurie said airily. "That was ages ago." *Why did Jane have such a fantas-*

tic memory? she wondered as she inserted the key into the lock and opened the door. Jane probably even remembered exactly how many pieces of glass they'd picked off the street!

Once inside, the girls took off their jackets. Laurie got a couple of sodas from the refrigerator and brought them into the living room. Handing one to Jane, she sat down next to her on the sofa and began flipping through the newspaper until she found the classified section.

"Here we are—'Help Wanted,' " she said cheerfully.

While Jane sipped her soda, Laurie ran her eye down the columns of listings. "Here's one!" she exclaimed. "Listen to this—'Part-time receptionist, doctor's office, three days a week.' "

Peering over Laurie's shoulder, Jane read the rest of the ad aloud: " 'Excellent computer skills a must.' "

Laurie frowned. "Hmmm—I wonder if they'd settle for 'barely adequate'?"

"How about this one?" Jane jabbed her finger at an ad headed "Salespersons Needed."

Laurie read the details. " 'To sell beauty products. Must have own car and be free to travel the East Coast.' "

"You could always drop out of school," Jane suggested hopefully.

Laurie made a face. "Yeah, right. There must be *something* here I could do!" But all the employers seemed to want either full-time help, a college degree, or five years' experience.

"I told you, you wouldn't find anything," Jane said, sounding smug. "It's not too late to go back to school and audition, you know."

Suddenly a small ad caught Laurie's eye, and she felt a surge of hope: " 'Song-A-Grams. Man or woman with good singing voice and outgoing personality to deliver greetings weekday afternoons and Saturdays. Costumes provided. Call Marjorie Vincent at 555–0790.' "

Glancing at the ad, Jane said, "It says 'man or woman.' "

"Well, what am I?" Laurie demanded, leaping to her feet and racing over to the phone. "A cocker spaniel? It's fate! I just know this is the job I'm meant to get!"

She quickly punched the number and held her breath. On the third ring, a woman answered. "Song-A-Grams! We delight your friends and confound your enemies!"

Laurie was so excited that her voice squeaked. "May I speak to Marjorie Vincent?"

"This is she," the woman replied. "What can I do for you?"

"I'm calling about your ad in today's paper, the one for a singer," Laurie said eagerly.

"How old are you?" Ms. Vincent asked suspiciously.

"I'm sixteen," Laurie told her, "and everyone says I have a really good voice—I was Maria in *The Sound of Music* at Chilton High last year. I even taught myself to play the guitar for the part."

There was a long pause. "Sorry. I don't think I could use someone that young," Ms. Vincent said at last.

"But I'm very dependable. Ask anybody!" *Except Matt Harding,* Laurie added mentally.

Another long pause. "Do you have your own transportation?"

"Oh, yes," Laurie assured her. Her tenspeed bike had a flat tire, but that was a minor problem.

"I really don't think this is the right job for a high-school girl," Ms. Vincent said politely but firmly. "Thanks for calling but—"

"Ms. Vincent," Laurie cut in, "will you at least write down my name and number in case you change your mind?"

The woman reluctantly agreed, and Laurie recited her name and phone number. But as they hung up, she got the distinct impression that Ms. Vincent was planning to toss the information into the nearest wastebasket, if she had even written it down at all.

Jane stood up and put on her jacket. "I'll be seeing Ms. O'Connor first period tomorrow morning," she said brightly. "I'll tell her you couldn't make tryouts today, but you'll be auditioning tomorrow right after school."

Laurie was too depressed to respond. She just waved a vague good-bye as Jane let herself out. When Jane had gone, Laurie found herself staring at a photograph of her brother on the mantel. Tom had laughed himself nearly sick when she announced that she was going on Operation Save. The idea of his bubble-brained kid sister raising that kind of money struck him as hilarious.

Although Laurie knew Tom loved her dearly, he simply couldn't take her seriously.

"But I'm *not* an airhead!" Laurie told the photograph. "Aunt Missy thinks I'm old enough to be responsible, and I'm going to prove it to you and to Jane. I'm going to find a job *today!*"

Filled with new energy, she reached for the paper again, but now it was buried under a large orange ball of fur. "Amber, how do you always manage to plop yourself right in the middle of everything?" Laurie scolded the sleeping cat just as the phone began to ring.

That's probably Mom reminding me to start supper, she thought. Picking up the receiver, she said, "Hi, Mom."

There was a brief pause. "Is this Laurie Adams?" asked a woman's voice. It was definitely not Laurie's mother.

"Yes—yes, it is," Laurie replied, feeling like a world-class idiot.

"Laurie, this is Marge Vincent from Song-A-Grams," the woman said, and Laurie gave a little gasp. "I've been thinking about your qualifications, and I'd like to talk to you in person. Could you stop by around four o'clock tomorrow afternoon?"

Laurie wanted to jump up and down and yell, "Yes! Yes! Yes!" but somehow she managed to keep her tone mature and dignified as she said, "Four o'clock would be fine."

"Good. I'll look forward to meeting you."

After Ms. Vincent told her the address, Laurie replaced the receiver in a calm manner. But she couldn't keep the lid on. "Hallelujah!" she shouted, waking Amber, who leaped into the air and landed with her back arched and her fur standing on end.

Scooping up the cat in her arms, Laurie danced around the living room and whirled until she was dizzy. Then she collapsed onto the sofa. Giddy with excitement, she began singing another of her favorite songs from *My Fair Lady* to her startled cat.

" 'Wouldn't it be loverly? Lover-ly, lover-ly . . . !' "

Chapter Two

The next afternoon, Laurie scowled at the clock on the front wall of her algebra classroom. It had to be broken! The last time she looked, it said 2:55. Now, hours later, it said only 2:56. Would the bell ever ring?

Laurie had been preparing for her interview with Ms. Vincent all day long, beginning with the outfit she'd selected that morning. She hoped the soft blue wool dress, high heels, and her mother's pearls really made her look more grown up. Laurie had even styled her usually unruly hair in a sophisticated pageboy. The result was definitely not the typical Chilton High look. The

girls stared and the boys made smart re-
marks, but Laurie just smiled mysteriously
and let them wonder what she was up to.

From the corner of her eye, she could see
Jane two aisles away, trying to get her attention by making weird gestures and mouthing
words. She seemed to be saying, "Miss the
corner and warm the slide into prom time,"
but that didn't make any sense at all.

Suddenly the bell rang. Laurie shot out of
her seat and was halfway to the door when
she heard Jane calling, "Laurie, wait up! I
have something to tell you!"

Laurie braked to a stop. *What's the matter
with me?* she thought. *My appointment isn't
until four!* Giving Jane a sheepish grin, she
said, "Sorry—I didn't mean to run out on
you."

"No problem," Jane said. "I know you're all
excited about the interview. I just wanted to
tell you that Ms. O'Connor asked me to be
the prompter for the show!"

"Hey, neat!" Laurie was really happy for
her. Jane was kind of shy and reserved, so
it would probably do her good to work with
the nutty bunch of extroverts in the drama
club.

"I have to pick up a copy of the script," Jane went on. "Will you come to the auditorium with me? I mean, I'm not even a member of the club, and you are, and you know all the kids."

Laurie hesitated. Going to the auditorium without auditioning would be like going to a fancy restaurant to watch everybody else eating fabulous food.

"It'll only take a few minutes. Please?"

"Okay," Laurie said at last. "I'll go with you. But don't think I'm going to change my mind about trying out, because I'm not." As they began walking down the hall, she eyed her friend suspiciously. "You didn't by any chance tell Ms. O'Connor to twist my arm a little?"

"Of course not!" Jane was the picture of injured innocence. "She understands how you feel about Operation Save. Besides, I heard that she's already picked somebody else to play Eliza Doolittle."

Laurie felt as if she had just swallowed a rock, but she tried to sound unconcerned. "Really? Who?"

"They say Elaine Desmond has it for sure," Jane said casually.

Laurie made no comment, but the rock sank to her stomach and turned into a boulder. True, Elaine had a nice voice, and she was beautiful, but unfortunately Elaine knew it. She was a real prima donna, and Laurie felt sorry for the other kids in the play who would have to put up with her.

When Laurie and Jane entered the auditorium a few minutes later, they found mass confusion onstage. Three boys were pushing a piano into place while Ms. O'Connor tried to keep order among the aspiring actors and actresses clustered around her. Suddenly one of the girls noticed Laurie's arrival. She quickly spread the word, and several of Laurie's friends from drama club hurried off the stage to welcome her. Jane, looking like the cat that had swallowed the canary, scuttled away to find a copy of the script.

"Are you here to try out?" Meg Stockwell asked eagerly.

"Oh, please say you are!" another girl chimed in.

Laurie shook her head. "No, I'm not. I really can't."

"It's not too late," Dan Evans told her.

"Elaine was called back for a second audition, but she hasn't been cast yet."

"If she plays Eliza, we're doomed!" said Judy Burns. "She acts like she's royalty or something."

While Laurie's friends pleaded with her, she couldn't help noticing what was happening onstage. A boy sat down at the piano and began playing the introduction to "The Rain in Spain," and a moment later, Elaine stepped forward and launched into the song under Ms. O'Connor's watchful eye. But Elaine's own green cat's eyes were riveted on Laurie, radiating waves of jealousy and resentment.

She thinks I'm here to take the part away from her, Laurie thought in dismay. *And that's exactly what Jane had hoped I'd do. The traitor! I never should have come.*

"I have to go," she said quickly. "Tell Jane I'm getting my coat, and then I'll meet her in the hall."

"Don't let Miss Rain in Spain chase you away," Meg begged. Giggling, she added, "Elaine's insane, but mainly she's a pain!"

That made Laurie smile, but it didn't slow down her flight from the auditorium. She raced to her locker as fast as she could in her two-inch heels, put on her coat, then returned to the auditorium doors, glancing at her watch. It was almost three-thirty. Her interview with Ms. Vincent was only half an hour away. Where was Jane? What was taking so long, anyway?

Just then Jane burst into the hallway, clutching the script. "Sorry—I didn't make you late for your appointment, did I?" she asked breathlessly. Laurie scowled. "Not yet. I'd give you a lecture on double-crossing friends, but I don't have time. My bike's out back—just wish me luck."

"You know I do," Jane said, squeezing her hand. "Call me the minute you get home, okay?"

Laurie nodded, then ran down the hall to the back entrance. Riding her bike in heels was tricky, especially with stubborn patches of ice still on the streets, but nothing was going to stop her today.

The cold air almost took Laurie's breath away as she stepped through the door. Lowering her head, she hurried toward the bike rack in the corner of the schoolyard. When she looked up, she saw someone in a dark red jacket and hiking boots, sitting on the bike rack, his shoulders hunched against the cold. Laurie felt a touch of panic as she recognized Matt Harding. She noticed that there were only two bicycles in the rack, her own and another one opposite it, and guessed that the second bike was Matt's.

But what's he doing sitting out here all alone in the cold? she wondered nervously.

Matt stood up as Laurie approached, and she came to a sudden halt, frozen in place by his icy stare.

"It's really nice of you to stop by," he said sarcastically.

"I—I don't know what you mean," Laurie stammered.

"Then I suppose you don't know that you chained your bike to mine!" Matt roared, rattling the chain she had hastily looped around the rack that morning.

Laurie felt her heart plummet into her size-nine pumps. "Oh, no!" she groaned. "Tell me I didn't do that! Matt, I'm so sorry! I don't know what I was thinking about."

"What do you care?" Matt gave a harsh laugh. "It's only about thirty degrees out, and I'm late for work, that's all. No big deal.

Now, will you cut out the apologies and unlock that chain?"

Laurie scrabbled frantically through the junk in her purse while Matt fumed. At last her fingers closed over the key. *Please let it open fast,* she pleaded silently as she bent down and jammed the key into the padlock. But naturally the key didn't want to turn.

"Here, let me do that," Matt snapped, snatching the lock out of her hand. Magically the key turned, the padlock opened, and with a sharp yank, he removed the chain that bound his bike to Laurie's.

"Matt, if you get in trouble at work, I'll be glad to explain what happened," Laurie faltered.

Matt pulled his bike from the rack and gave her a withering glare. "Just do me one favor," he said. "From now on, stay as far away from me as you can!" Then he mounted his bike and raced off.

"I'm really sorry," Laurie whispered to his disappearing back. She felt tears welling up in her eyes as she got on her own bike and began pedaling toward the street. Somehow she would have to cheer herself up before her interview, or she'd never get the job. Ms.

Vincent wouldn't be interested in hiring a messenger who sang "Happy Birthday to You" with tears in her eyes.

Don't think about Matt, Laurie told herself as she rode down Main Street. *Just think about Operation Save. Think about working with a lot of other kids who are doing something good for this world. Think about helping those little children on St. David.*

She was beginning to feel more like herself again by the time she reached the outskirts of Chilton. Soon a colorful poster at the side of the road told Laurie that she had reached the offices of Song-A-Grams. Getting off her bike, she wheeled it up the long driveway that led to an old white farmhouse and leaned it against the porch. Then, assuring herself that she was perfectly calm, Laurie climbed the porch steps and lifted the brass knocker.

"*Please* make her like me," she breathed as she heard someone unlocking the door.

When it opened, Laurie wasn't prepared for the vision that appeared. A gypsy fortune-teller dressed in a blinding assortment of colors with heavily made-up eyes and long jet black hair peered at her as though she were a crystal ball.

"Hi! You must be Laurie Adams," the gypsy said. "I'm Marge Vincent. Come on in."

Trying not to stare, Laurie followed her through the entrance hall into what appeared to be a combination office, music studio, and wardrobe closet.

"Just relax for a minute, Laurie, while I get out of this costume." Ms. Vincent waved vaguely toward a green overstuffed chair. "I just got back from a delivery."

Laurie took off her coat and perched on the edge of the chair as Ms. Vincent vanished into another room. Her gaze wandered to the exotic array of costumes along one wall, including a policeman's uniform, a football jersey and helmet, a cowgirl outfit complete with ten-gallon hat, a gorilla suit, a clown costume, and a hula skirt. Laurie could picture herself ringing somebody's bell and bursting into song as a cowgirl, a policeman, or even a clown—but a gorilla? The thing looked as if it weighed a hundred pounds!

"Well, that feels better!" Marge Vincent, who turned out to be an attractive young woman with tousled blond curls and laughing eyes, breezed through the door and dropped into a swivel chair behind the desk. "It's nice to meet you, Laurie."

"Same here. I mean, it was nice of you to let me come," Laurie mumbled.

Ms. Vincent got straight to the point. "So, what makes you think you want to get into this crazy business?"

Swallowing hard, Laurie said, "Well, I have to raise quite a bit of money for a summer work project in the Caribbean, and I saw your ad, and I really love to sing, and—well, I think this is the job I'm meant to get."

Ms. Vincent's eyebrows rose. "The job you're meant to get?"

Laurie nodded eagerly. "I know I'm meant to go to St. David to help rebuild a schoolhouse for the kids, so I'm sure this job is meant for me, too."

"I see." But Ms. Vincent didn't quite look as though she did. "What do your parents think about your applying for a job like this?"

"They think it's kind of strange," Laurie admitted, "but they told me to go ahead with the interview."

"I see," Ms. Vincent said again. "Well, let's

hear you sing." Getting out of her chair, she went over to the piano and ran her fingers over the keys. "Do you know 'My Bonnie Lies Over the Ocean'?"

Laurie nodded, joining her at the piano. "Sure."

"Okay." She thrust a sheet of paper into Laurie's hands and sat down at the keyboard. "This is a song I set to that tune for a farewell party tomorrow afternoon. Why don't you give it a try?"

While Ms. Vincent played an introduction, Laurie hastily scanned the unfamiliar words, then began to sing.

" 'You're leaving, and oh, how we'll miss you . . .' "

As she got the feel of the song, she began to add some fancy vocal flourishes and finished with a dramatic crescendo, arms outstretched. " 'Good-bye, good-bye, you'll always be welcome back home!' "

Letting her arms drop to her sides, Laurie waited anxiously for the verdict.

Ms. Vincent stared at her as though she were an alien who had just dropped through the roof. "That's quite a voice you have, young lady. How old did you say you were?"

"Sixteen," Laurie replied.

"Hmmm . . ." Ms. Vincent frowned, and Laurie felt her hopes fading fast. But they revived as the woman said, "Well, let's go ahead with the interview. You've got the voice, all right, but singing is only one part of the job. You have to be an actress, too. Let's pretend I'm the guest of honor at the farewell party, and you show me how you would deliver that song. This time you'll be singing without accompaniment—there won't be a piano when you deliver a Song-A-Gram."

Laurie smiled. Acting came as naturally to her as singing. Laying the sheet of paper on the piano, she prepared to give an award-winning performance.

Startled, Ms. Vincent asked, "Don't you need the lyrics?"

"I know them already," Laurie assured her. "If only I could memorize my schoolwork as fast as I learn song lyrics and dialogue, I'd be valedictorian of my class."

Laurie thought Ms. Vincent looked impressed, but all she said was, "All right, let's try it. You've come to the house, and you walk into the room where the guests are. Now what do you do?"

Picturing herself arriving at the height of a farewell party, Laurie gazed mournfully into Ms. Vincent's eyes. " 'You're leaving, and oh, how we'll miss you,' " she sang. " 'It pains us to tell you good-bye . . .' " She clutched both hands to her heart. " 'We'll try to be brave as we kiss you . . .' " (Loud lip-smacking) " 'But later we'll sit down and cry.' " Laurie mopped a flood of imaginary tears.

" 'Good-bye, good-bye, please think of us where e'er you ro-o-oam.' " She dropped to one knee in a pleading gesture. " 'Good-bye, good-bye, you'll always be welcome back home!' "

As she sang the last line, Laurie jumped up and wrapped her arms around her prospective employer in a giant bear hug. Then, embarrassed by how completely she'd thrown herself into the act, she stepped back quickly. Had she overdone it?

Ms. Vincent was studying her with that peculiar expression on her face again, as though Laurie had suddenly turned green and sprouted antennae. At last she said, "Laurie, that was incredible! You're a natural-born ham!"

"That's what my brother calls me—among other things," Laurie said, grinning.

Ms. Vincent began wandering around the cluttered room, muttering distractedly to herself.

Turning back to Laurie, she said, "What kind of transportation do you have?"

"A ten-speed," Laurie said brightly.

Ms. Vincent rolled her eyes. "Laurie, you can't do this job on a bike! You'll be wearing a costume."

"Yes, I know." Laurie beamed at her. "I figure I could decorate my bike and put a Song-A-Grams sign on it! Everybody would notice the costume and read the sign. It would be great advertising for your company, and it wouldn't cost you a cent!"

Sinking into her swivel chair, Ms. Vincent shook her head in wonder. "Laurie Adams, what am I going to do with you?"

"Hire me?" Laurie asked hopefully, crossing her fingers for luck.

After what seemed like a year, Ms. Vincent finally said, "Tell you what. I can pay twenty dollars per delivery. If your parents say it's okay, be here at three-thirty tomorrow, and we'll see if you have what it takes."

"Yes!" Laurie shouted. Then, belatedly remembering to act like a calm, professional woman, she added, "Thank you very much, Ms. Vincent. You won't be sorry, I promise you!"

Chapter Three

Laurie's throat was dry as she pushed the elevator button in Tracy's Department Store the following afternoon. Glancing up at the clock above the bank of elevators, she saw that it was almost four-thirty, time for her to deliver her first Song-A-Gram. Mr. James Thornton, the store manager, was moving up to company headquarters, and his farewell party was being held in the employee lounge on the third floor.

Luckily, the store had requested an official-looking messenger instead of an Arabian Nights genie or a hula dancer, so Laurie's jacket, slacks, and cap didn't draw much attention from the customers. She was grateful that the long pants hid her trembling legs as she stepped into the elevator.

This is no time for panic, she told herself firmly, straightening her bow tie and tugging at the visor of her cap. *Just do it. Ms. Vincent is counting on you, remember, and you're counting on this job.* But as the elevator carried her upward, she had the uncomfortable feeling that her stomach was still on the first floor.

When the door slid open at the third floor, Laurie got out and started down the hall as though she were walking the plank over a pool filled with sharks. She could hear laughter and other party noises coming from a room at the far end of the corridor, so she headed in that direction.

The closer she got to the door, the more nervous she felt. Laurie's stage fright usually disappeared the minute the curtain went up, but acting and singing right in the middle of the audience would be an entirely new experience. She was seriously considering forgetting the whole thing when the door opened and a smiling young woman drew Laurie into the crowded room.

"You're right on time," she said. "I'm Charlotte Smith, Mr. Thornton's secretary. That's him over at the refreshment table, the one in the dark blue suit."

Laurie stared at the tall man for a moment, unable to move.

"Go get him!" Ms. Smith urged, giving her a gentle push.

Remember Operation Save, Laurie thought. Squaring her shoulders, she marched over to the guest of honor. "I have a message for Mr. James Thornton," she said loudly.

He turned to look at Laurie in surprise, and the crowd immediately gathered around them. With a captive audience to entertain, Laurie suddenly felt her nervousness melting away. She forgot her trembling knees and threw herself into her act just the way she had yesterday for Ms. Vincent.

The laughter began the minute Laurie clasped Mr. Thornton's hands and gazed soulfully into his startled face. A few people tossed paper napkins for her to use as handkerchiefs when she pretended to weep, and everyone broke up when she dropped down on one knee, pleading to be remembered.

When Laurie reached the grand finale and

threw her arms around the manager, the crowd applauded and cheered. Laurie knew her face was scarlet, and Mr. Thornton was blushing even more than she was. But he was also grinning from ear to ear.

"Punch and cake for the messenger," he announced. "She's almost convinced me to stay!"

"That was great!" Ms. Smith exclaimed, and gave her a hug. Then she dragged Laurie to the refreshment table, gave her a plate heaped with sandwiches and cake, and handed her a glass of punch. To her amazement, Laurie was an instant celebrity, and she soon discovered that it wasn't easy to juggle a plate and a glass when you were surrounded by admirers who kept patting you on the back and wanting to shake your hand.

Somehow Laurie managed to finish her food. But as she was edging toward the door, Ms. Smith stopped her before she could leave. "This is for you," she said, slipping a five-dollar bill into her hand.

Laurie stared at the money in confusion. "Uh—thanks, but my boss didn't say anything about taking tips . . ."

"Keep it," Ms. Smith insisted. "You were

super. And you can tell your boss that there are a lot of people here who will be using Song-A-Grams from now on!"

Laurie floated down to the first floor as though the elevator were a magic carpet. Every dollar she earned brought her closer to St. David and Operation Save!

When she reported back to the office, Ms. Vincent was delighted with Laurie's debut as a Song-A-Gram messenger. She told her that she had the job, and that Laurie could keep any tips she was offered. Ms. Vincent also assured her, in answer to Laurie's hesitant question, that a two-hundred-fifty-pound neighbor answered all calls for the gorilla.

By the end of the week, Laurie felt like an old pro. She had made two more deliveries and put sixty-five dollars in the bank toward her registration fee for Operation Save. Jane was impressed when Laurie told her about it on the phone Friday evening.

"Sixty-five dollars already! That's unbelievable!" she exclaimed.

"It is, isn't it?" Laurie agreed happily. "Ms. Vincent said she probably wouldn't have a delivery for me every afternoon, but so far I haven't missed a day. Yesterday was Mr. and Mrs. Collins's fiftieth wedding anniversary. They're crazy about cats, so I went as a big black cat with long whiskers and a humongous tail." She giggled. "They were so thrilled that they made me wait until they could bring their two Persians to hear me sing!"

Jane giggled, too. "That must have been fun!"

"And then today there was a party for Mr. Yeats at the bank," Laurie went on. "He's retiring to Texas, so I got to wear the cowgirl outfit. I played my guitar and sang the special lyrics Ms. Vincent wrote to 'Home on the Range.' "

"How did you carry the guitar on your bike?"

"*Very* carefully," Laurie said. "But I may have a real problem tomorrow. I'm supposed to be a hobo clown for some little kid's birthday party, and I have to deliver a bunch of balloons, too."

"Sounds tricky," Jane said.

"Oh, I'll handle it. For twenty dollars, I can handle anything!" Changing the subject, Laurie added, "So what's happening with you? You haven't told me how *My Fair Lady* is going."

"Okay, I guess," Jane replied. "I mean, this

is the first show I've ever worked on, but everything seems to be going fine."

"That's good."

Laurie tried to sound enthusiastic, but she couldn't help feeling disappointed that they were getting along so well without her. Jane started talking again, but Laurie wasn't really listening. *Life would be perfect,* she thought, *if I could just stop thinking about the musical—and about Matt Harding.* In spite of the fact that he avoided Laurie as if she were a contagious disease, Matt kept popping into her thoughts at odd times, like now.

". . . But Elaine the pain is driving everybody up the wall," Jane was saying when Laurie tuned back in. "Well, good luck with the clown bit tomorrow, and be careful on the bike."

"I will," Laurie promised.

That promise came back to haunt her the next afternoon as Laurie rode her bike to Ms. Vincent's office. She suspected she was in for trouble when she noticed huge black clouds filling the sky. Then Ms. Vincent announced that Laurie's assignment was Bobby Desmond's birthday party. Since there was only one Desmond family in town,

Bobby had to be Elaine's little brother. Last but not least, the clown costume was much too big. When Laurie put it on, the sleeves hung three inches past her fingertips, and the pants were far too long and baggy.

While Ms. Vincent was filling the balloons with helium from a tank, Laurie found some bright-colored ribbons and wrapped them around the legs of her costume so she could ride her bike. The final touch was her makeup—clown whiteface; a huge, gloomy mouth; and a big red nose. Laurie tucked her hair up under a scraggly orange wig and topped it with a battered hat with a floppy brim. She looked so ridiculous that she had to laugh at her reflection in the mirror.

"Laurie, I'm not sure you're going to be able to manage on your bike," Ms. Vincent said, peering out the window at the overcast sky. "It looks like we're in for a storm. I'd better drive you in the car."

"No, really, I'll be okay," Laurie said quickly. She knew her boss had a lot of work to do in the office. Besides, Laurie wanted to show Ms. Vincent how competent and responsible she was. "If I have any trouble, I'll let you know."

Before Ms. Vincent could protest, Laurie grabbed the bunch of balloons and hurried out to tie them to the handlebars of her bike. Then, checking to make sure the Song-A-Grams sign was in place, she pedaled off down the driveway, keeping one eye on those threatening clouds.

The Desmonds lived on the other side of town, and Laurie was scheduled to appear at two o'clock, just as the birthday boy was about to cut his cake. She didn't want to be late, but every time she tried to pedal faster, the balloon strings began to tie themselves into hopeless knots. As Laurie wheeled through the center of town in her outlandish costume with the balloons streaming behind her, everyone who saw her grinned and waved. She couldn't let go of the handlebars to wave back, but she smiled and nodded her head to return their good-natured greetings.

Laurie was relieved when she turned down Maple Lane. It was a quiet street with no traffic to dodge. And even though a chill breeze had started to blow and the clouds were still hanging overhead, with any luck before they burst she would arrive at the Desmonds.

Laurie was approaching weird old Mr. Allerton's place when the breeze suddenly gained force, nearly tearing her wig and floppy hat from her head. As Laurie made a frantic grab for the wig with one hand, the bunch of wind-driven balloons took control of her bike, aiming it straight at the huge boulder that marked the end of Mr. Allerton's driveway. Before Laurie could react, the bike hit the rock, and she found herself hurtling through space. Her teeth jarred together as she pancaked on the ground like a plane without landing gear.

For a long moment, Laurie lay perfectly still, her eyes squeezed shut, gasping for breath. Then, very slowly, she opened her eyes and discovered that she was on a merry-go-round—the trees and the sky were whirling around in gigantic, dizzying arcs. Laurie clung to the ground to keep from falling off the earth until the merry-go-round finally slowed to a stop and the world came back into focus.

She felt a dull, throbbing ache in the back of her head as she squinted down at herself. Two arms, two legs. Good! Nothing seemed to be missing. Then she caught sight of her bike and groaned. The front wheel was folded in half like an omelet. Mr. Allerton's boulder was wearing the Song-A-Grams sign, and her balloons were bobbing around in the bare branches of a nearby maple. Laurie gazed in despair at the mess as a large raindrop splashed against her cheek.

"Hey, down there! Are you all right?" a voice called out. A moment later, Laurie heard the pounding of footsteps as somebody raced toward her down the driveway. Raising her aching head, she wondered if she was having a hallucination, because the person who was running her way looked very much like Matt Harding.

Laurie quickly closed her eyes. This had to be a bad dream! But when she peeped cautiously from under her eyelids, there was Matt, bending over her. Oh, why did he always have to show up when she was in the middle of a catastrophe?

"Laurie? Is that you?" Matt asked, kneeling next to her. "I saw you fall. Are you all right? Is anything broken?"

"I—I don't think so," Laurie mumbled. Her ribs hurt and her back hurt and so did her elbows and knees, but as much as she wanted to, she didn't dare cry. Her clown makeup would streak all over her face.

Matt sat back on his heels and scowled at her, his concern replaced by irritation, now that he knew she was still alive. "How on earth did you get yourself into this mess?" he asked.

Slowly Laurie raised herself to a sitting position and groaned as every aching muscle screamed in protest. "I was on my way to deliver a Song-A-Gram at Bobby Desmond's birthday party," she said. "I'm supposed to be there in a few minutes, but I ran into that rock. And now my bike is wrecked, and the balloons are up a tree, and . . . and . . ." She couldn't finish her sentence because unshed tears were forming a big lump in her throat.

"You could have broken your neck!" Matt pointed out angrily. "Who cares about the bike and the balloons!"

"*I* care," Laurie cried. "I have to get to my job!"

"Are you sure you're all right?" Matt asked as he got to his feet.

Laurie nodded. She felt another couple of raindrops.

"Okay. If Gramps will let me use his car,

I'll drive you. Don't move," Matt ordered. "Stay right there till I come back."

Laurie stared after him as he strode back up the drive, too stunned even to thank him for his offer. Was Matt really friendly with Mr. Allerton? Gramps was Chilton's most notorious character. With his wild white hair and straggly beard, he always looked angry, and when anyone dared to set foot on his property, he would chase them away, yelling and waving his cane like a war club. Little children loved to scare themselves with stories about how mean and evil the old man was.

Laurie was debating whether or not she should try standing up when she suddenly heard a strange rumbling noise. Afraid that the storm was about to break, she glanced at the sky. Then she realized that the sound she was hearing came from the elderly car that was sputtering down the driveway with Matt at the wheel. It was an ancient Model A Ford in perfect condition, its black paint-work gleaming as though it were brand-new.

The car clanked to a stop beside her, and Matt got out. Folding his arms, he surveyed the scene of the disaster. "I think I can reach the balloons if I stand on the roof," he mumbled.

Matt pulled off his boots and climbed from the running board to the hood and then to the roof in his stocking feet. "Gramps will kill me if I scratch the paint," he explained to Laurie.

As she watched, wide-eyed, the rain began in earnest. "Get into the car!" Matt shouted. "No use both of us getting soaked."

Laurie scrambled to her feet and made a dive for shelter. Once inside, she could hear Matt's footsteps through the drumming of the rain above her head. Moments later she saw him jump to the ground with a cluster of balloons in one hand and pick up his boots with the other. Laurie leaned over to open the door on the driver's side, and Matt tossed in the shoes, then thrust the balloons inside and got in himself.

Chapter Four

Matt was soaked, all right. Water poured down his face from his hair and dripped off his chin as he glared at Laurie. "So you're going to the Desmonds. That's on Oak Drive, right?" he muttered.

Laurie nodded. "Yes. They're expecting me at two o'clock. What time is it now?"

Glancing at his watch, Matt said, "Two-fifteen." He put the car in gear, and it jerked forward.

Laurie bit her lip. What if when she got to the party, they sent her away because she was so late? How would she ever face Ms. Vincent? And what about her bike? Laurie wanted to ask Matt if he thought it could be repaired, but she decided against it. From the grim expression on his face as he tried to see the road through the sweep of the windshield wipers, she was afraid he might bite her head off.

He looks as if he's chiseled out of rock, Laurie thought. *I wonder if he ever loosens up.*

And then she noticed that the corner of Matt's mouth was twitching, almost as though he was trying to keep from smiling.

"Laurie Adams," he said, "you are something else. You're a disaster looking for a place to happen!"

Under her clown makeup, Laurie could feel her face turning red. "I guess I am," she admitted sadly.

"Does this go on all the time, or just when I'm around?" Matt threw a quick glance in her direction, and Laurie thought she actually saw a twinkle in his blue eyes.

"I guess you inspire me," she sighed. "I really lead a fairly normal life most of the time."

At that, Matt threw back his head and laughed. Laurie couldn't believe her ears.

Here he sat, soaking wet in his stocking feet, driving her through a rainstorm that would have discouraged Noah, and he was laughing as though it were the biggest joke in the world!

When he had sobered up enough to speak, Matt said, "You probably consider it a 'normal' day if nobody winds up in the emergency room." Then more seriously, he added, "Tell me something, Laurie. Why did you take this weird job anyway?"

"Because I need the money."

"What for? I'd really like to know."

He seemed so genuinely interested that after a moment's hesitation, Laurie told him all about Operation Save and how much it meant to her. By the time she finished, they were pulling up in front of the Desmonds' spacious split-level house.

Matt stopped the car and looked at Laurie with new respect in his blue eyes. "That's pretty cool," he said quietly. "There aren't many people who would work so hard to help others. Good luck, Laurie."

"Thanks," she murmured, flushing with pleasure. Then, glancing out the window through the driving rain at the Desmonds' house, she added nervously, "Well, I guess it's now or never."

"You'd better straighten your wig," Matt suggested, trying to keep a straight face. "And I think your nose is about to fall off."

"Oh, no!" Laurie fumbled with the elastic that held both wig and hat in place, then gingerly pressed the red bulb in the middle of her face. She hadn't given a thought to how she looked since she had been launched into orbit over the handlebars of her bike. Now she realized that her costume was caked with dirt and all her carefully tied ribbons had come undone.

"What am I going to do?" she wailed. "I'm a total mess!"

"Just pretend you're supposed to look that way," Matt suggested cheerfully. "The kids won't know the difference."

But Elaine will, Laurie thought. *I don't want her to see me like this!* She wished she could duck down and hide under the dashboard, but she couldn't back out now. Even if the Desmonds refused to let her perform, she had to at least make the effort.

"I guess I don't have any choice," she said aloud, gathering up the tangled balloon strings.

Matt reached across to open the door for her. "I'll wait for you," he promised.

Laurie smiled gratefully at him and struggled out into the storm. Water was flowing down the front steps of the house like a miniature Niagara Falls as Laurie pressed the doorbell. Would anyone be able to hear it over the pounding of the rain?

Just then a maid in uniform opened the door. *Thank goodness it's not Elaine!* Laurie thought. "Song-A-Gram for Bobby Desmond," she said as brightly as possible.

The maid looked astonished, but she let Laurie into the entrance hall. "I'll tell Mrs. Desmond you're here," she said, and left Laurie to drip on the carpet.

"Well, look what the cat dragged in!"

Laurie cringed as Elaine walked into the hall, looking like a model in designer jeans and a white turtle-neck sweater. In comparison, Laurie felt grubbier than ever.

"Hi, Elaine," she said, hoping her voice didn't reveal how miserable she felt.

"You're late," Elaine snapped. "Bobby's already cut his cake."

"I'm sorry," Laurie said stiffly. "I had some problems getting here."

Glancing out the window by the door, Elaine raised her eyebrows. "I see you've traded your bike for a Model A. Since when are you and Gramps Allerton such good friends?"

Laurie was saved from making an explanation by the return of the maid, who said, "Come this way, please. The children are in the family room."

Well, at least they didn't kick me out, Laurie thought as she stumbled along behind the maid. Elaine brought up the rear of the parade.

The family room was on the lower level of the house. Laurie could hear the children's happy chatter as she started down the stairs. But suddenly her feet seemed to be locked in place, and as she teetered on the step, Laurie realized that she was standing on the baggy legs of her costume. Before she could free herself, she lost her balance and plunged headlong down the three remaining steps. She landed on her hands and knees, still clutching the bunch of balloons. Behind her, Laurie could hear Elaine's delighted snicker.

Laurie's head was spinning, but she

glanced up quickly. The children were sitting around the party table, staring at her in startled silence. Worse yet, Mrs. Desmond was recording the whole scene on her video camera. *What do I do now?* Laurie wondered, panic-stricken. Then she remembered what Ms. O'Connor always said during play rehearsals: If you make a mistake, don't stop. Pretend it's part of the action and keep right on going.

Laurie crawled on all fours over to a little girl sitting at one end of the table and tugged at the child's party dress. "Are you Bobby Desmond?" she asked in a squeaky voice.

The children started to laugh. "That's not Bobby!" one of them shouted.

Pretending to be annoyed, Laurie crawled on to the next child, a little boy who was already giggling in anticipation. "Are *you* Bobby Desmond?" she demanded. This time, all the children yelled, "That's not Bobby!"

They grew more and more excited as Laurie edged her way around the table from one child to another, pretending to look for Bobby. When she finally reached the head of the table where the birthday boy was seated, they were almost hysterical with glee.

"Are *you* Bobby Desmond?" she gasped as though she were exhausted by her search.

"Yes! *That's* Bobby!" the children shrieked, and Laurie hoped her eardrums might stop vibrating in a couple of weeks.

"Well, thank goodness I found you!" she squeaked. "Where have you been hiding?"

"I was right here all the time!" the little boy said between giggles.

"I have something for you," Laurie announced. Taking Bobby's hand, she led him to the center of the room. As the other children crowded around him, she realized that the whole Desmond family had gathered to watch the fun. Ignoring Elaine's scowl, Laurie began her song, handing Bobby the balloons one by one as she sang.

"One is when our Bobby walked.
Two, he started in to run.
Three, he rode a hobbyhorse,
Four, a bike was lots of fun.
Five, he swam across the pool,
Six, he trotted off to school.
Seven, that boy's no one's fool.
Now he's eight, he's really cool.
Happy birthday, Bobby!"

The children cheered and clapped and Bobby was grinning from ear to ear. Delighted, Mrs. Desmond tried to persuade Laurie to have some cake and ice cream, but she shook her head.

"Thank you very much," she said, "but someone's waiting for me in the car." *At least, I hope Matt's still waiting,* she thought.

"I'm so sorry you can't stay. We really enjoyed your song," Mrs. Desmond said, smiling warmly at Laurie. "Elaine, will you please show this wonderful clown to the door?"

Elaine tossed her head and started up the steps. Laurie stumbled after her, still tripping over her baggy pants. But she pretended it was all part of the act, waving to the children and blowing kisses as she went.

As soon as her mother was out of earshot, Elaine sneered, "Honestly, Laurie, I can't *believe* you'd give up even a *small* part in the show to take a stupid job like this, wearing those awful costumes and making a fool of yourself for a bunch of little kids!"

Laurie knew that trying to explain Operation Save to Elaine would be like discussing Einstein's theory of relativity with a hamster. If Elaine had ever done anything for anybody in her whole life, it was the world's best-kept secret. Instead, she asked, "How's the show going?"

"Perfectly, of course!" Elaine snapped.

They had reached the front door, and Laurie peered out anxiously through the rain, relieved to see that the old car was still there. "Well, guess I'll see you around," she said brightly. "Good luck with *My Fair Lady*."

Elaine looked confused for a moment, as if she thought there had to be some nasty meaning hidden in Laurie's words. Laurie just gave her a cheerful wave and sloshed out into the storm. Her costume soaked up water like a sponge, and by the time she opened the car door, it felt as though it weighed a ton.

Laurie had expected to find Matt fuming with impatience, but he was sitting there calmly with his head back and his eyes closed, almost as if he were sound asleep. As she scrambled into the car, Matt opened his eyes and smiled at her so warmly that Laurie found it hard to believe this was the same Matt Harding who had told her to stay as far away from him as she could get.

"How'd it go?" he asked, starting the engine.

"Pretty well, all things considered," Laurie said. Looking down at her sodden, dirty costume, she added sadly, "I just hope I don't lose my job. I bet Ms. Vincent will tear all the fur off King Kong when she sees this costume! And then there's my bike—if it can't be fixed, I won't be able to deliver Song-A-Grams even if she doesn't fire me."

Although the sky was clearing and the rain had slowed to a sprinkle, clouds of gloom were gathering in Laurie's head. If she lost her job, there was no way she could ever raise the rest of the money for Operation Save in the next two weeks.

As Matt began driving down Oak Drive, he said, "Let's go back to Gramps's place and take a look at that bike. Maybe it's not as bad as it looks."

A few minutes later Matt stopped the car in front of Mr. Allerton's house. He got out, and Laurie followed him over to where her mangled bike lay. Matt picked it up and studied the damage.

"You know, Laurie, there's nothing really wrong with this except the front wheel," he said at last. "If you buy a new wheel and a tire, I could put them on in no time. And the handlebars need to be straightened, but I can do that with a wrench. Do you have any money? We could go to the bike store right now."

"All the money I've earned so far is in the bank," Laurie told him. She was beginning to feel a little more hopeful. "But maybe Ms. Vincent will pay me today when I report in"—then her spirits took a sudden nosedive—"unless she cuts my pay for ruining this outfit, that is."

Matt eyed her thoughtfully. "There's nothing wrong with it that a washing machine won't fix. It's not ripped or anything, just muddy. Come on—I'll drive you to her place."

As they got back into the Model A, Laurie said, "But won't Gramps be mad at you for taking his car out again?"

Matt smiled and shook his head. "He knows I'll bring it back when we're through. He's really a nice guy, you know."

Laurie *didn't* know. Were they talking about the same person? Gramps Allerton, who scared little children to death? But come to think of it, Matt himself seemed so different today. Maybe she had been wrong about Mr. Allerton, too.

From that point on, everything seemed to straighten itself out, largely due to Matt. He helped Laurie explain about the accident to Ms. Vincent, who wasn't at all concerned about the clown costume. She was just relieved that Laurie hadn't been hurt. When Laurie had changed into her regular clothes and washed the clown makeup off her face, Ms. Vincent paid her in full, telling Laurie that she had received a phone call from Mrs. Desmond raving about the hilarious clown.

Grateful that her job was secure, Laurie was even more grateful to Matt. After he drove her to the bike shop where she promptly spent her day's pay on a used front wheel, a new tire, and a tube, they went to Matt's house. It didn't take him long at all to replace the twisted wheel, put on the new tire, and straighten out the handlebars. When he hung the Song-A-Grams sign over the rear fender and stepped back so Laurie could see the results, she almost burst into happy tears.

"Oh, Matt, I don't know what I would have done without you!" she exclaimed. "How can I ever thank you?"

He studied her face so intently for so long

that Laurie felt herself beginning to blush. "I'll have to think about that," he said softly. "I'll let you know." Then he climbed back into the Model A.

Laurie stared after the ancient car as it chugged off down the street, and she kept thinking about Matt all the way home on her bicycle. What had he meant when he said he'd let her know how she could thank him? For one split second back there, Laurie had almost thought he was thinking of kissing her.

But that was crazy. No one had ever seen Matt Harding with a girl, although he could have dated any girl at Chilton High. He didn't come to the school dances, and he didn't participate in any extracurricular activities, like clubs or athletic teams. He always seemed to be alone, and he disappeared the minute classes were over for the day.

Yes, Matt Harding was a mystery, all right. Would Laurie ever figure him out?

Chapter Five

Clinging tightly to her tray, Laurie edged through the crowd in the school cafeteria. It was crammed with kids, and the roar of two hundred voices along with the clatter of dishes and trays was deafening, but Laurie didn't really notice. She was too depressed.

It's Friday already, she thought dismally as she headed for a table with two empty seats, *and I've only had three Song-A-Gram deliveries all week.*

Last night Laurie's aunt Melissa had phoned to see if she had raised her registration fee for Operation Save yet, and Laurie had to confess that she still needed seventy-five dollars. She felt like crying when her aunt mentioned that there was another girl just dying to take Laurie's place. She had only one more week to raise that money, and that meant she had to make four more deliveries.

Lost in her worries, Laurie didn't pay attention to where she was going. Her foot caught on a table leg, and she fell into an empty chair, managing to catch her milk carton before it skidded off her tray and hit the floor. She looked around for Jane, who had been right behind her a minute ago. It was eerie the way Jane managed to drop out of sight.

While Laurie saved a seat for her friend, she gave herself a pep talk. *Everything's going to be all right. You'll make the money in time. Ms. Vincent has a delivery for you tomorrow, remember, and that means you'll only have fifty-five dollars to go.*

But the worry just wouldn't go away. Laurie closed her eyes, and her shoulders slumped. Maybe she wasn't meant to go on Operation Save, after all. Maybe it was just a foolish dream. Against her closed eyelids, the vision of St. David began to fade into the sunset.

Then Laurie gave herself a little shake and opened her eyes. She'd never get through the day if she didn't stop stewing about that registration deadline. Once again she scanned the cafeteria for Jane, who was still nowhere in sight. But then Laurie's gaze was caught by a group at the next table. Elaine Desmond was holding court, surrounded by her usual crowd of hangers-on. It looked as if she were telling a story, and the other kids were listening with rapt attention. Occasionally one of them would glance across at Laurie and snicker.

Laurie felt her stomach tightening. It didn't take ESP to know that Elaine was talking about her, probably giving her pals a stumble-by-stumble account of Laurie's performance at Bobby's birthday party.

Suddenly Jane appeared and slammed her tray down on the table. "I wish I were seven feet tall!" she sputtered, sinking into the chair next to Laurie's. "When you're as short as I am, nobody sees you. They just cut in the line in front of you as if you were invisible! A person could starve to death that way!"

Glancing at her loaded tray, Laurie smiled. "It doesn't look as if you're going to starve today."

"It's a good thing, too," Jane said, digging into her chow mein. "I need all the strength I can get. What a week! Thank goodness it's Friday."

"Why? What's wrong?" Laurie asked, putting her own worries aside for the moment.

Jane heaved a huge sigh. "It's the musical. I don't see how it's ever going to be ready in three weeks." Noticing Elaine, she lowered her voice and leaned close to Laurie. "Elaine knows all the songs, but she can't remember her lines from one day to the next. All the other kids have their parts almost completely memorized, but I have to prompt Elaine on every other word! She can't even remember where she's supposed to stand, or when she's supposed to move. She's driving everybody bananas!"

"Try not to let it get you down," Laurie said, forcing a note of encouragement into her voice. "Elaine's not a quick study, but she gets it straight eventually." She didn't mention that Elaine also had a habit of blowing her lines at the most dramatic moments during a performance. Jane would find that out soon enough.

"Well, I'd feel a lot better if she'd just get

one sentence straight," Jane groused. "And so would Ms. O'Connor. She's about ready for the funny farm."

As Laurie took a bite of her sandwich, she glanced over at Elaine's table again. It looked as if she was taking up a collection from her friends—they were all handing her coins or bills, which she stuffed into her purse. When Elaine stood and picked up her tray, the others did, too. Then she held up her hand for silence and whispered a few words. The whole group whooped with laughter and turned to look at Laurie as they followed Elaine toward the door.

"I wish I knew what she was up to," Laurie muttered, scowling. "I wonder why Elaine dislikes me so much. I've never done anything to her."

"It's because she knows she doesn't have half the talent in her whole body that you do in your little finger," Jane said loyally. "And she also knows that if you'd tried out for *My Fair Lady*, she'd never have gotten the lead in a million years. Not only that, but I bet she found out that Mr. Clemens picked you to sing a solo on Parents' Night. Elaine's just jealous—forget about her."

Laurie shook her head. "I wish I could, but I can't. I'm absolutely sure she's cooking up some trouble for me, and I have more than enough problems without any help from her."

"No work?" Jane asked sympathetically.

"Nothing since Tuesday. I have one delivery for tomorrow, but I'd feel a whole lot better if I had one today, too."

"I *told* you, you should have tried out for the show," Jane said with a sigh. "Now it's too late, and if you can't come up with enough money for Operation Save—"

Laurie clapped her hands over her ears. "I don't want to hear this! I won't give up. I'm going to make it!"

"Okay, okay," Jane said hastily. "Forget I mentioned it." Changing the subject, she asked, "So how are things going with you and Matt Harding?"

Laurie finished her sandwich, groping for an answer. Although Matt was always tiptoeing around in the corners of her mind, she hadn't spoken to him all week. Every time she went to her locker, she looked around hopefully, but no Matt.

"They're not," she said at last, hoping she

sounded casual. "I didn't really expect to hear from him. I mean, just because he was nice to me last Saturday doesn't mean he ever wants to see me again."

Jane gave her a skeptical look. "And that doesn't bother you at all, huh?"

"No, it doesn't!" Laurie stood up and snatched her tray.

"Don't get mad, Laurie," Jane pleaded.

Feeling ashamed of herself for snapping at her best friend, Laurie sighed. "Sorry—I don't mean to be such a grouch. I guess I'm just uptight today."

Jane smiled. "That's okay. I understand. Well, see you in algebra, I guess. Who knows, maybe Ms. Vincent will have a job for you later today."

Laurie's afternoon classes seemed endless. When the final bell rang, she made a record-breaking dash to the pay phone in the main hall. Dropping a quarter into the slot, she punched Ms. Vincent's number, begging silently, *Please have a job for me. Please, please, please!*

Ms. Vincent sounded breathless when she answered. "Oh, Laurie, I'm so glad you called! A customer just stopped by wanting a Song-A-Gram delivered as soon as possible. I'm writing the lyrics right now, but I won't have time to deliver it myself. Can you get here right away?"

Laurie's spirits rose like one of Bobby Desmond's helium-filled balloons. "I'll be there in a flash!" she cried. Hanging up the phone, she ran to her locker, humming a happy tune. *With twenty dollars today and another twenty tomorrow, I'll be up to a hundred sixty-five,* Laurie thought as she grabbed her jacket and stuffed her books into her backpack. *That means I'll only have to make thirty-five dollars next week!*

Matt wasn't at his locker, and his bike wasn't in the rack when Laurie came outside, but she told herself she didn't care. So what if he was gorgeous, and could even be nice once in a while? Laurie had a lot more important things to think about than a boy who had obviously forgotten she was alive.

As she pedaled at top speed toward Ms. Vincent's office, Laurie sang out loud, practicing the number she would be performing tomorrow for the policeman who had been chosen Chilton's "Officer of the Year." The mayor, the police chief, and members of the city council would all be there when Laurie sang her tribute, dressed in a convict's uniform.

I wonder what I'll be wearing this afternoon, she thought, turning her bike down Ms. Vincent's driveway. *And I sure hope it's a short song—I won't have much time to learn it.*

"My goodness! You certainly got here fast," Ms. Vincent said, looking up from her desk as Laurie burst in the door. "It seems as if I just hung up the phone!"

Laurie laughed. "I was so glad you have a job for me that I practically flew. Where am I going, and what's the occasion?"

"Do you know a Mr. William Allerton?" Ms. Vincent asked.

Startled, Laurie said, "You mean *Gramps* Allerton?"

"Yes, I believe that's what they call him. Anyway, it was his granddaughter who stopped by. Today's his ninetieth birthday, and I've just about finished a song for him. Why don't you get into your costume, and then we'll run over it together."

"Okay. What am I wearing?" Laurie asked a little nervously. She wasn't sure she liked the idea of delivering a Song-A-Gram to the town's leading eccentric, but a job was a job.

"Well, Mr. Allerton's granddaughter requested a hula dancer," Ms. Vincent told her. "I know it's a little chilly for that, but apparently the old man has fond memories of when he once lived in Hawaii."

Laurie almost groaned aloud. Although last Saturday's storm had melted the snow and warmed the air considerably, Chilton, Massachusetts, wasn't exactly Honolulu. But she didn't complain.

Think about the twenty dollars, Laurie told herself as she changed into a flowered halter and grass skirt. *You'll be that much closer to going on Operation Save.* She briefly considered taking off her sneakers and socks, but even though they looked ridiculous with the rest of the outfit, Laurie knew she couldn't ride her bike barefoot, so she kept them on.

After tucking a large artificial hibiscus behind one ear and draping several paper leis around her neck, she joined Ms. Vincent at the piano to run over the song. The lyrics were set to the tune of the old Hawaiian folk song "Aloha Oe," and Laurie had no trouble memorizing them. Then she sang the song a few times, trying to imitate the graceful arm and hand movements of a hula dancer, but her nerves were twanging like the strings of a ukelele.

The ukelele strings were still vibrating when Laurie rode her bike up Gramps Allerton's driveway a short while later. In spite of what Matt had said about how nice Gramps was, the old stories kept running through her mind. What if Matt was wrong? What if Gramps met her at the door, waving his cane and yelling? What if he had an attack dog that would tear her limb from limb before she had a chance to sing a note?

The house was hidden from the road by the huge oaks that surrounded it, so Laurie had never actually seen it before. Now that she had, she caught her breath in surprise. Instead of the creepy Victorian mansion she had imagined, it was a gracious old colonial home, probably dating from the 1700s.

As Laurie propped her bike up on its kickstand, she could feel her teeth starting to chatter. She wasn't sure whether it was from nerves, the cool breeze, or both, but she climbed the front steps and eyed the brass knocker with dread.

Well, what are you waiting for? she asked herself. *Go ahead before you freeze to death out here!*

Squaring her bare shoulders, Laurie lifted the heavy knocker and let it fall twice.

Nothing happened. There wasn't a sound from inside the house. *Maybe Gramps isn't home,* she thought hopefully. Laurie was tempted to get back on her bike and leave, but knowing that if she didn't deliver her message, she wouldn't be paid, she knocked twice more.

While she waited, Laurie gazed around uneasily. The front and sides of the house were bordered with well-tended evergreen shrubs, but toward the back she could see what appeared to be animal pens. Were her eyes playing tricks on her, or was that really a skunk she saw in one of them? And what kind of strange animal was that in the next pen?

Laurie was so absorbed in wondering about the menagerie that she didn't realize someone had opened the door until he spoke.

"Laurie, what on earth are you doing here?"

Amazed, Laurie jerked around to see Matt Harding standing in the doorway. He did not look pleased to see her.

Raising her chin in the air, Laurie said haughtily, "I've come to deliver a Song-A-Gram to Mr. Allerton. Is he home?"

Matt frowned. "Yes, he's here." He hesitated for a moment, then said without much enthusiasm, "I guess you'd better come in."

Laurie followed him through the entrance hall into a big living room. She couldn't help staring at her surroundings. Although she knew next to nothing about antiques, she guessed all the Early American furniture must be pretty valuable.

And then she saw Gramps Allerton. He was sitting at a chessboard on a small table in front of the fireplace, and his fierce gray eyes under beetling brows peered at her intently, taking in every detail of her costume from the hibiscus in her hair to the sneakers on her feet.

Finally, "Well, what is it, young lady?" he asked.

Laurie swallowed hard, trying to get her heart out of her throat, and managed to force a weak smile. "I—I have a Song-A-Gram for you," she croaked.

The old man stared at her. "A *what*?"

"A message—a singing message," Laurie explained. Before she lost what nerve she had left, she launched into her song and dance.

> "*Aloha oe,* it's your big day,
> *Mele kahana hale* on your birthday!
> At ninety years, you're . . ."

Laurie's voice died away as Gramps leaped out of his chair, roaring like a wounded elephant. "Ninety years!" he bellowed. "I am *not* ninety years old! It's not even my birthday! Is this some kind of practical joke?" He snatched up his cane, waving it like a saber. "Didn't anyone ever teach you respect for your elders?"

Laurie stared at him in horror. He wasn't ninety? It wasn't his birthday? Then why had his granddaughter ordered a message for his ninetieth birthday?

"I'm so sorry, Mr. Allerton," she whispered. "I thought—I mean, I was told . . ." Choked by tears of humiliation, Laurie turned and ran out of the room, through the front door, and down the steps to her bike.

Matt followed her, shouting, "Laurie, wait!"

But she couldn't bear to face him now. Laurie was about to mount her bike when Matt's strong hands clamped down on the handlebars. Unable to move, Laurie stared at the ground through tear-dimmed eyes. Why couldn't he just let her go home and hide in her room forever?

"Laurie, look at me," Matt demanded.

Slowly she raised her head and met his eyes.

"Why would you play such a stupid trick on Gramps?" he said angrily. "I didn't think you were like that. What's he ever done to you?"

Matt's words were like a slap in the face, and now Laurie's misery was replaced by rage. "It wasn't a trick!" she snapped. "I was just doing my job. Mr. Allerton's granddaughter ordered the Song-A-Gram this afternoon, and Ms. Vincent sent me to deliver it!"

"Gramps doesn't have a granddaughter," Matt snapped back.

"Doesn't have a granddaughter?" Laurie echoed incredulously. "Then who . . .?"

Suddenly she knew. It had to be Elaine Desmond! That was what all the giggling and whispering was about in the cafeteria, and why Elaine had been collecting money from her friends! She must have gotten permission to leave school early so she could drive to Ms. Vincent's place and order the Song-A-Gram in person.

Laurie was about to tell Matt that Elaine was the culprit, not she, but the look of contempt on his face stunned her into silence. Even if she had been able to find words, it wouldn't have made any difference. Since Matt actually believed she was capable of deliberately tormenting an old man, nothing Laurie could possibly say would convince him she was innocent.

Furious and deeply hurt, Laurie wrenched her bike out of Matt's grasp, leaped onto the seat, and pedaled as fast as she could down the drive.

Chapter Six

Two days later, Laurie's footsteps echoed and reechoed down the main corridor of Chilton High. Uneasily she glanced over her shoulder. Could someone be following her? An empty school on a Sunday afternoon was spookier than a haunted house on Halloween.

Of course, it wasn't completely empty. Mr. Clemens and the members of the school chorus he directed were rehearsing their Parents' Night program in the auditorium, but Laurie was pretty sure she was the only person walking the halls.

Unless somebody *was* following her. Could it be Matt?

No way, Laurie thought, shaking her head. She had seen him on her way to the school a few minutes ago, and he had waved frantically at her from the sidewalk as she whizzed down Main Street on her bike, but Laurie had ignored him. Whatever Matt wanted to say to her, Laurie didn't want to hear. She knew what he thought about her, and his angry words still rang in her ears.

Eager to put Matt out of her mind, Laurie entered the auditorium and hurried down the aisle to the front. Mr. Clemens was seated at the piano, and several kids from the chorus were gathered around him.

"Glad you could make it, Laurie." The director beamed at her, his eyes sparkling over his Ben Franklin glasses. "I'm sorry to drag you over here on a Sunday, but this will be our only chance to run through your solo in the auditorium before tomorrow night."

"I don't mind, Mr. Clemens," Laurie said. "I wasn't doing anything except homework, anyway."

"I've turned the mike on," Mr. Clemens told her. "Why don't you go up onstage and try it so we can check the volume."

As Laurie climbed the steps to the apron

of the stage, she tried to forget that right behind the closed curtains was the set for *My Fair Lady*. She tapped the mike, then counted aloud as Mr. Clemens fiddled with the controls. Finally satisfied, he sat back down at the piano, positioned some sheet music on the rack, and began to play the introduction.

Laurie smiled down at him and at the chorus members sitting in the front row. She loved the song she was about to sing—the words were positive and upbeat, and today she really needed a lift.

Looking out over the rows of empty seats, Laurie pictured the audience that would be smiling back at her the following night. Then suddenly her eyes widened. There, sitting in the very last row, was Matt Harding.

What's he doing here? she thought nervously. *When did he come in? Was he following me in the hall just now?*

Laurie took a deep breath to calm her racing heart and lifted her chin defiantly. No matter what Matt thought of her, she refused to hang her head as though she were guilty when she wasn't.

The introduction ended, and Laurie began

to sing, giving the song everything she had: " 'Something good is going to happen to you, Happen to you this very day . . .' " As she sang, she couldn't help looking at Matt. She could see that he was listening intently, but his expression was unreadable.

When the last note died away, the kids gave her an enthusiastic round of applause, and Mr. Clemens said, "Laurie, that was just beautiful! You almost made me cry."

"Thanks, but don't you think we ought to go through it one more time?" Laurie asked. She was hoping to put off the moment when she would have to face Matt, who hadn't moved from his seat.

But Mr. Clemens said, "Oh, no, Laurie, that won't be necessary. Your performance was absolutely perfect. Don't change a thing. Just be here tomorrow night at seven."

As slowly as she could, Laurie left the stage. She paused to chat with some of her friends, then began walking up the center aisle. Matt had disappeared, but Laurie was pretty sure he'd be waiting for her outside in the hall.

She was right. He was leaning against the wall opposite the auditorium doors when she came through them. Laurie stood still, fixing Matt with a level gaze as he walked over to her. There was a long, uncomfortable silence. Matt finally broke it, and his voice was husky when he spoke.

"I want to apologize for those things I said to you the other day, Laurie," he said. "I'm real fond of Gramps, and when he got upset, I got upset, too. I know you'd never hurt anybody intentionally." A flicker of a smile touched his lips. "Accidentally, maybe, but certainly not on purpose. Do you think you can forgive me?"

Laurie let out her breath in a sigh of relief. "Thanks for saying that, Matt," she said softly. "Of course I can forgive you." Stretching out her hand, she added, "Friends?"

Matt's smile broadened as he took her hand. "Friends."

"Is Gramps all right?" Laurie asked anxiously. "I felt just terrible about the whole thing. I was afraid he might have a stroke or something."

"Oh, he recovered pretty fast. Then I talked him into calling Ms. Vincent, and she told him the same thing you did—that some girl saying she was his granddaughter had placed the order for the Song-A-Gram," Matt said. "Do you have any idea who that might have been?"

Do I ever! Laurie thought grimly. But tattling on Elaine wouldn't make any difference now, so all she said was, "I think I do, but I'd rather not say."

Matt shrugged. "Suit yourself. Anyway, after he calmed down, Gramps decided that it was kind of funny. He wants to see you, Laurie, so he can apologize for the way he acted."

Realizing that they were still holding hands, Laurie blushed. She pulled her hand from his and smoothed her hair nervously. "I don't know, Matt," she said. "It took all my courage to knock on his door the first time. I don't know if I could bring myself to do it again so soon. Maybe after a little while, like in a week or so . . ."

"He wants to see you now, Laurie. Today," Matt insisted. "Just for a few minutes, okay?" He grinned. "I'll come with you and I promise I won't let him holler at you or poke you with his cane."

"Well—okay." Laurie smiled weakly. "But I can't stay long. We have company coming for dinner." Luckily, that was the truth, and it gave her a good excuse to leave if Gramps should decide to throw another tantrum.

"No problem. I'll drive you. I have the Model A," Matt said as they began walking toward the side door that led to the parking lot.

"But what about my bike?" Laurie worried.

"Leave it in the rack. I'll drop you off back here after we visit Gramps, and you can pick it up then."

"You have an answer for everything, don't you?" Laurie teased.

Matt unlocked the doors of the old car, and they both climbed in. "Not everything," he said seriously, sliding behind the wheel. "Just some things." As he started the engine, he looked over at Laurie. "You know, that song you sang was really great. You have a fantastic voice."

Laurie smiled. "Thanks." She felt a warm glow inside. For as long as she could remember, people had complimented her on her voice, but somehow it was extra special to hear those words from Matt.

From the corner of her eye, she watched his face as he drove out of the parking lot and down the street. As if he had felt her gaze, Matt glanced at her and smiled, but the smile didn't reach his eyes.

"Is something wrong, Matt? You look worried."

His smile faded. "I am. I'm worried about Gramps. I think there's something wrong with him."

"Is Mr. Allerton really your grandfather?" Laurie asked.

Shaking his head, Matt said, "No, he's no relation, but he's probably my best friend in the whole world."

That puzzled Laurie. Although Matt's eyes were on the road, he seemed to read her mind. "I know what you're thinking. Why don't I have friends my own age instead of hanging out with an old man?"

"Well, yes, as a matter of fact," she confessed. "But I guess it's none of my business."

"I want it to be your business, Laurie. If we're really going to be friends like we said, you need to know some things about me." He paused, and Laurie saw a muscle twitch in his cheek, as though it was hard for him to go on.

"My family's been having a really hard

time lately," Matt said at last. "My dad was hurt in a bad auto accident last year. He may never be well enough to work again. He gets just enough from disability to keep us going, but that's about all. Mom can't get a job because he has to have someone with him all the time. The only money we have for clothes or extras is what I earn. So I work at the grocery store and try to make as much as I can on the side mowing lawns or trimming trees or shoveling snow—anything I can get."

Laurie's heart ached for him. "Oh, Matt, I didn't realize that," she said softly. "But the kids at school don't care if you have money or not. They'd still like to be your friends."

Matt shot her a wry glance. "Laurie, you don't know what it's like to have friends when you don't have money. It's always 'Let's go get a pizza' or 'Let's go to the movies.' But I know that if I buy that pizza, my kid brother won't have a notebook for his science project. And if I take a girl to the movies, we might not be able to pay the gas bill."

Laurie had never thought about it before, but now that she did, she realized how lucky

she was. Even though her parents sometimes complained about the cost of Tom's
college tuition, her family had never needed
to count every penny. Laurie's own problems
earning enough money for Operation Save
suddenly seemed insignificant compared
with Matt's struggle to provide for his family.

"Everyone's nice about it," Matt continued.
"When you tell them you're broke, they offer
to pay your way. But you can't let them do
it when you know you won't be able to return the favor. It's easier just to forget about
making friends and keep your mind on your
work."

Laurie had a sudden inspiration. "What
about the Youth Center?" she suggested.
"That's free."

There was no humor in Matt's laugh.
"Think about it, Laurie. They don't charge
admission, but almost every week there's
some activity that costs money. They're having a party, so everybody brings refresh-
ments. Or they're going bowling at five
dollars a person. Or they're chipping in for
a gift or something."

Now that Matt had pointed it out to her,
Laurie realized it was true, and she won-

dered for the first time how many other kids stayed away from the Youth Center for that very reason. "You're right!" she exclaimed. "I'm on the program committee, and at our next meeting, I'm going to insist that we plan some activities that won't cost a cent!"

"Don't make any changes on my account," Matt said stiffly.

Laurie knew that she had wounded his pride and decided it was time to change the subject. "You haven't told me about Gramps," she reminded him. "How did he become your best friend?"

Matt relaxed a little. "I got to know him last year when I began mowing his lawn and doing some yard work for him. Then I found out he had a kind of refuge for wounded animals behind the house. He takes care of them until they're well again, and then he turns them loose." Smiling, he added, "Of course, they don't go very far away. They still hang around, looking for handouts. That's why Gramps always chases little kids off his property. He's afraid they'll try to pet the animals and get bitten or something."

"Really?" Laurie was amazed. "And all the time I thought he was just being mean."

"Mean?" Matt laughed. "Gramps has a heart like a marshmallow! When I told him I've always wanted to be a veterinarian, he put me in charge of his zoo. I've set a sea gull's broken wing and patched up an old tomcat who was on the losing end of a fight. Now we've got a skunk with a bad cut on his paw and a raccoon with a broken leg, and we've just adopted some orphaned baby rabbits."

"That is so neat!" Laurie exclaimed.

They were pulling into Gramps's driveway now, and instead of dreading her meeting with the old gentleman, she was actually looking forward to it.

"Anyway," Matt went on, "Gramps is really something. He used to be a college professor, and he's always finding sneaky ways to teach me things. He's an expert at chess, and he has a terrific stamp collection. He's taught me to play chess well enough to give him a real battle, and now he's teaching me about stamps."

"I can understand why he's your best friend," Laurie said. "He sounds like quite a guy."

She was about to ask why Matt thought

there was something wrong with Gramps when he stopped the car in front of the house. "I'll show you our menagerie before we leave," he promised as they got out. "But now, let's go see Gramps."

Laurie followed him up the steps. Matt opened the door without knocking and called out, "We're here, Gramps. Here's your hula dancer!"

Blushing to the roots of her hair, Laurie hung back as they entered the living room. When he saw her, Gramps struggled to his feet with the aid of his cane. His white beard didn't conceal a welcoming smile. "Aloha, young lady," he said.

Laurie bit her lip. "Oh, Mr. Allerton, I hope you can forgive me for that mistake about your birthday!"

The old man waved her to a chair. "That wasn't a mistake. Somebody set you up deliberately. Any idea who it was, or why?"

"Yes, I do," Laurie said. "I'm just sorry you had to be involved."

"And I'm sorry I flew off the handle the way I did," Gramps replied. Then he chuckled. "At least it cost the villain some money to make trouble for you."

Laurie smiled. "Thank goodness Ms. Vincent insisted on payment in advance!"

Turning to Matt, Gramps said suddenly, "Judges, chapter four, verse nineteen."

Laurie stared at him. What was he talking about? He wasn't making sense. She knew that Judges was one of the books in the Bible, but what did that have to do with anything? Maybe the old man was losing his mind, and that's why Matt was worried about him.

She was even more confused when Matt quoted promptly, " 'Give me, I pray thee, a little water to drink; for I am thirsty.' "

"Very good, Matthew." Gramps beamed at him. "But instead of water, how about lemonade for all of us? There's a pitcher of it in the refrigerator."

As Matt left the room, Laurie realized that the old gentleman was perfectly sane. For some peculiar reason, these two had developed a kind of secret code based on Bible verses. She was dying to know why, but before she could ask, Gramps had a question for her.

"Now why do you think this person was trying to embarrass you?"

"I'm not really sure," Laurie admitted. "She has a grudge against me for some reason. My friend Jane says it's jealousy."

"Song of Solomon, chapter eight, verse six," Gramps said solemnly. At Laurie's puzzled look, he quoted, " 'Jealousy is cruel as the grave.' "

Matt came back with glasses of lemonade and a plate of cookies on a tray. As he set it on the coffee table, he said, "Isaiah, chapter twenty-two, verse thirteen."

" 'Let us eat and drink,' " Gramps quoted.

Laurie couldn't contain her curiosity any longer. "Do you both know the whole Bible by heart?"

Grinning at her, Matt said, "I think Gramps does, but I've been learning a few verses to throw back at him. It's like a game we play—Gramps says it's a good way to train the memory."

"An excellent way," the old man agreed. "But enough about our little game. I want to hear more about this work project of yours, Laurie. Matt tells me you're planning on helping rebuild a school somewhere in the Caribbean."

Laurie was more than happy to talk about

her favorite topic, and before she knew it, she was chattering away. "And I only need thirty-five dollars more for the registration fee," she finished breathlessly.

Gramps leaned back in his chair and beamed at her. "Operation Save sounds like a very worthwhile endeavor. You should be very proud of yourself." Chuckling, he turned to Matt. "What do you think, Matthew? Might this young lady turn into a real Hawaiian Missionary?"

Matt started to laugh, too, and Laurie looked from one to the other, trying to figure out what was so hilarious. Were they referring to her hula costume, or was this yet another of their private games?

Seeing her confusion, Matt explained, "That's a stamp collector's joke, Laurie. Hawaiian Missionaries are among the most valuable stamps in the world."

"I didn't know missionaries had their own stamps," Laurie replied, still puzzled.

"They don't," he told her. "But when Hawaii first issued stamps back in 1851, it was the missionaries who wrote most of the letters and used most of the stamps."

"Well, if I were a missionary, I hope I'd be

a good one," Laurie said, smiling. "But I'm afraid I wasn't a very good Hawaiian."

"Quite the contrary." Gramps's eyes were twinkling. "In fact, on my eighty-fourth birthday in November, I hope you'll come back and sing to me again."

"I'd like that," Laurie said, and she meant it.

"Well, it's time for my nap now," Gramps said. He began to struggle to his feet. Matt quickly stood up to help him and handed him his cane. "Thank you for coming to see me today, Laurie. Come back soon—don't wait until November," he added.

Laurie noticed the look of concern on Matt's face as the old man slowly shuffled out of the room. "He never used to get so tired," he told her softly. "Now he gets out of breath after just a few steps. I wish I knew what's wrong with him."

"Has he been to a doctor?"

Matt shook his head. "He won't listen to me when I've tried to get him to go. But his daughter is coming down from Boston to-morrow. She'll make him see the doctor whether he wants to or not. She bosses Gramps around as if she were his mother instead of his daughter." He sounded as though he didn't like the woman very much.

"Well, I guess that's okay as long as she can get him to go," Laurie said hesitantly.

"I guess." Matt reached for her hand. "Come on—time for that visit to the Allerton zoo."

Laurie felt a tingle all the way up her arm as Matt's hand closed around hers. Walking beside him through the house to the back door, she realized that although Matt's good looks had attracted her at first, there was so much more to him than just a handsome face. He was proud, strong, capable, and loyal. *And I think I just may be falling in love with him,* Laurie thought.

Matt led her outside. Beyond a small walled garden were the pens she had noticed on her first visit to Gramps's house. The rabbits were comfortably housed next to a big, scruffy tomcat, who looked like a pirate with a patch over one eye. In another pen, a raccoon was trying to climb out of his food dish, and in yet another was the skunk Laurie had glimpsed before. All the animals seemed happy to see Matt, and he had a gentle word for each of them.

As Matt leaned down to pet one of the rabbits, the others hopped forward, eager for their share of his attention.

"You really *should* be a vet, Matt," Laurie said. "You're so good with animals."

A look of pain crossed his face. "I try not to think about that, because it'll never happen. Gramps has offered to pay my tuition all the way through college and veterinary school, but I can't accept his help. My family simply couldn't manage without me."

Sometimes life just isn't fair, Laurie thought sadly.

But Matt wasn't the kind of person to dwell on his misfortunes for very long, and soon they were both laughing at the raccoon's antics.

As he drove Laurie back to school to pick up her bike, her heart was singing. Whoever would have thought earlier in the afternoon that she and Matt would end up being friends? And perhaps one day they would be something more. . . .

Chapter Seven

"Good-bye, Laurie! Come back and sing for us again real soon!"

"We had such a wonderful time! Thank you!"

Smiling and waving, the elderly ladies clustered in the doorway of the retirement home on Tuesday afternoon as Laurie blew them a kiss on her way to her bike. They had loved her Raggedy Ann costume with its full blue skirt and lace-trimmed pantaloons, and the thick braids of orange yarn that were attached to her white ruffled cap. But most of all, they had loved her singing. Usually Laurie delivered her Song-A-Gram and went on her way, but the residents were so delighted by her visit that she had stayed to conduct a singalong of old favorites.

As she pushed up the kickstand of her bike, she glanced at her watch. Ms. Vincent would think she'd decided to retire and move into the home herself! Carefully Laurie rolled up the legs of her pantaloons, revealing her red-and-white-striped stockings, and mounted her bike.

Pedaling down the street, she felt as though her wheels weren't even touching the ground. So far this week, everything was going her way. Laurie's solo on Parents' Night was a big success, she was about to be paid for the job she'd just finished, and she had another delivery scheduled for tomorrow. Unless something drastic should happen, she would have her registration fee for Operation Save in the mail three days before the deadline. Tom wouldn't dare to call her a bubble-brain now!

But what made Laurie happiest of all was her increasing closeness to Matt. She could hardly wait to tell him her good news. His warm smile really lit up her life. Now if only Laurie could convince him that it was possible to go out with a girl without spending any money. Matt didn't date because he seemed to think every girl expected to be taken to a movie or out to dinner, and Laurie was determined to prove he was wrong. She had already started making a list of things they could do that wouldn't cost a cent, and soon she'd have to start dropping hints.

As she coasted to a stop at a red light on Main Street, Laurie felt her pantaloons beginning to slip down her legs again. If she didn't roll them up, they would certainly get caught in the chain and she'd never make it back to Ms. Vincent's office. Once Laurie had edged her bike over to the curb and onto the sidewalk, she leaned it against a mailbox and bent down to deal with her problem.

Everyone who passed seemed to be enjoying the spectacle of Raggedy Ann rolling up her ruffles in the center of town. But Laurie was used to good-humored attention by now, and it didn't bother her a bit—until she stood up and saw Elaine Desmond come out of the drugstore on the corner and head toward her. As usual, Elaine looked as if she had just stepped off the cover of a fashion magazine in her oversized cream-colored sweater, coffee-colored leggings, and brown suede boots. She eyed Laurie's costume as though it were a reject from the local thrift shop.

"That's such an *adorable* outfit, Laurie," she sneered. "It really becomes you."

This was the first time the two girls had run into each other since the Song-A-Gram episode last Friday. Knowing that Elaine must be dying to know how her practical joke had turned out, Laurie decided that the best revenge would be to let her keep on wondering as long as possible. So she smiled and said cheerfully, "Thanks, Elaine. It's one of my favorites."

That was obviously not the reaction Elaine had anticipated. She frowned, then switched topics. Narrowing her eyes, she said, "I hear you were out with Matt Harding on Sunday. I didn't know you two were dating."

Laurie laughed. "I didn't know we were either!"

"You mean you *weren't* out with him on Sunday?"

"Oh, I didn't say that," Laurie replied airily.

Elaine was looking more confused—and more irritated—by the moment. Instead of continuing to beat around the bush, she tried a more direct approach. "So, Laurie, how's the job going? Somebody told me you delivered one of those singing message things to Gramps Allerton last week. That must have been a really *interesting* visit," she said with a self-satisfied smirk.

"Oh, it was." Laurie gave Elaine her most dazzling grin. "That delivery was the best one I've had so far. Gramps is so much fun when you get to know him! He's invited me to visit him again anytime I like."

Elaine's jaw dropped. She stood staring at Laurie, for once totally speechless, and the expression on Elaine's face was all the revenge Laurie needed.

But Elaine recovered quickly, and as Laurie started to walk her bike back onto the street, she called after her, "It's great that you're enjoying your job so much, Laurie. I guess that must almost make up for not having a part in the show."

Laurie's smile never faltered, even though Elaine's latest barb stung. She wheeled off down the street, leaving Elaine without a target. *How can someone so pretty be so mean?* she wondered.

But not even Elaine's nastiness could dampen Laurie's spirits for long. She wasn't about to allow anything to discourage her today.

After Laurie had collected her fee from Ms. Vincent and changed out of her costume, she hurried home. She had a lot of homework to do, but first she wanted to dash off a triumphant note to Aunt Missy, telling her not to let anyone else take her place on the Operation Save team. Laurie was sure her aunt would be every bit as happy about it as Laurie was herself.

In her bedroom, she tossed her backpack on the bed, then browsed through her collection of CDs, looking for the right background music to listen to while she wrote her aunt Missy. Almost automatically, she pulled out her *My Fair Lady* disc.

This is the real test, she told herself. *It's time to stop daydreaming about what might have been. If you can listen to it without aching all over, you know you've won.*

Laurie slipped the disc into her CD player and took a pad of stationery and a pen from her desk. As the music began to play, she propped herself up against the pillows of her bed. Amber jumped up and curled into a ball beside her.

Listening to the familiar overture, Laurie felt one sharp twinge of regret, but it passed quickly. Soon she was busily writing, humming along with the music without even thinking about it.

"Amber," she marveled to the cat, "it doesn't hurt anymore! I can actually hear the songs without feeling torn apart because I won't be singing them onstage!"

Amber responded with a bored yawn just as Laurie's father stuck his head in the doorway of her room to tell her that supper was ready.

"Be right there, Dad," she said. Laurie quickly put her letter into an envelope and addressed it, tucking it into her backpack to be mailed on her way to school in the morning, then went down to join her parents in the dining room.

After supper, Laurie was studying algebra at her desk when she heard the doorbell.

"Laurie, there's someone at the door. Can

you get it?" her mother called. "I'm washing my hair, and I don't know where your father is."

"Sure, Mom," Laurie called back. She slid off the bed and ran downstairs, thinking that it was probably Jane. Her friend had mentioned something in school about wanting company on her trip to the library that evening.

But when Laurie opened the front door, it wasn't Jane who was standing on the steps. It was Matt Harding, and one look at his face told her that something was very wrong.

"Matt, come in," Laurie urged. "You look terrible! What's happened?"

Matt stepped inside. "It's Gramps, Laurie. He's in the hospital. The doctor says he's in pretty bad shape. They're moving him to a hospital in Boston for surgery tomorrow."

"Tomorrow!" Laurie gasped. "Oh, Matt! Is it that serious?"

He nodded grimly. "He has to have a triple bypass. And then, when he recovers from surgery, he'll be going to stay with his daughter. She doesn't think it's good for him to keep living here alone." He swallowed hard. "I'm going to the hospital now to say good-bye to him. I thought maybe you might want to come with me."

"Oh, I do!" Laurie exclaimed. "Wait just a minute while I tell my mom where we're going."

She hurriedly explained the situation to her mother, then pulled on her jacket and joined Matt. As they walked toward Main Street, she said anxiously, "Now tell me everything, Matt, right from the very beginning."

"Well, Mrs. Lawrence—that's Gramps's daughter—arrived yesterday morning. She marched him off to the doctor, and Doc Miller checked him right into the hospital. As soon as they got the results of the tests, they started making arrangements for heart surgery in Boston. I found out about it when I stopped by after work today to say hi to Gramps and take care of the animals. Mrs. Lawrence was at the house, packing up his things."

Laurie's eyes widened. "You mean Gramps won't be coming back at all? Not ever?"

Matt shook his head sadly. "It doesn't look like it. She was packing all his clothes and his personal belongings, like his chess set and his stamp albums." In the light of a streetlamp they were passing, Laurie saw him frown. "Mrs. Lawrence doesn't like me. You should have seen the way she looked at me when I let myself into the house—like I was a thief or something. I just hope she won't try to stop us from seeing Gramps tonight."

"She wouldn't really do that, would she?" Laurie asked, distressed. "Do you know why she doesn't like you?"

Matt's frown deepened. "Oh, yes, she made it perfectly clear on her last visit. She thinks I only made friends with Gramps because of his money. She says everybody takes advantage of him because he's too generous for his own good." Then he sighed. "I guess I can understand why she feels that way. After all, he *is* her father, and I suppose she's just trying to protect him."

"But Gramps doesn't need protection from you!" Laurie said indignantly, puffing a little as she hurried to keep up with Matt's longer stride. "He's your best friend, and you're certainly his!"

"Mrs. Lawrence doesn't believe that," Matt muttered. "She thinks because I'm poor, I just hang around with Gramps hoping that when he dies, he'll leave me all his money. She's already petitioned the court to be named the conservator of his estate."

"What does that mean?"

"It means she's asking the court to decide that Gramps is senile and can't manage his own affairs, so the judge will give her the power to sign papers for him and take over his property and his bank accounts."

Laurie was horrified. "But Gramps isn't senile at all!" she protested. "There's absolutely nothing wrong with his mind!"

"We know that," Matt said, "but a lot of people in town think he's eccentric and weird. I'm afraid she'll get her way."

Laurie had to admit that he might be right. After all, until last Friday, she had been one of those people.

As they entered the hospital, she could see Matt squaring his shoulders, as if he were gathering his strength to face the formidable Mrs. Lawrence. Feeling increasingly nervous herself, Laurie followed him to the reception desk.

The receptionist eyed them coldly while Matt asked to see Mr. Allerton. "Patients in the cardiac unit are allowed only two visitors at a time," she told him, "and Mr. Allerton's daughter is with him now."

"That's all right, Matt," Laurie said quickly, touching his arm. "You go. I'll wait for you here."

But Matt wasn't about to give up. "Please, ma'am, he's being transferred to a hospital in Boston tomorrow, and he might never come back," he pleaded. "We're friends of his, and we just want to say good-bye. We'll only stay a minute, honest."

Laurie held her breath while the woman hesitated. Then, apparently touched by Matt's sincerity, she glanced over her shoulder to see if anyone might be listening and whispered, "I really shouldn't be doing this, but"—she slipped two visitor's passes into Matt's hand—"room two-oh-four."

"Thanks!" Matt whispered back. "Come on, Laurie. Let's go!"

Chapter Eight

The elevator carried Laurie and Matt to the second floor. As they hurried down the silent corridor to Gramps's room, Laurie almost expected an alarm to start shrieking, "Three visitors in room two-oh-four!"

Matt pushed open the door, and Laurie stuck close to him as he entered. She was definitely not looking forward to meeting Mrs. Lawrence, whom she pictured as a hatchet-faced harpy hovering over poor Gramps as he lay helpless in his hospital bed.

But to her surprise, Gramps was sitting up, looking as chipper as he had on Sunday.

His eyes lit up when he saw them, and he stretched out a hand to each of them, saying, "Matthew—Laurie! I'm so glad you came!"

The smartly dressed middle-aged woman on the far side of the bed sprang to her feet like a startled sentry. Laurie was even more surprised to find that she wasn't hatchet-faced at all. In fact, she was rather pretty, but the expression on her face was far from welcoming.

Before the woman could speak, Matt said quickly, "Mrs. Lawrence, this is my friend Laurie Adams. We just came to say good-bye to Gramps."

"But you're not going to rush away," Gramps insisted. To his daughter, he added, "Margaret, sit down and relax. A little visit isn't going to do me any harm."

"Did you give this boy a key to your house?" Mrs. Lawrence demanded.

"Yes, I did," Gramps said. "And I want Matthew to keep that key. I expect him to keep an eye on the house, tend to the yard, and take care of the animals until they're well enough to fend for themselves."

Mrs. Lawrence frowned. It was clear to

Laurie that she didn't think Matt could be trusted.

"And another thing, Margaret," Gramps went on, "I want Matthew to have my stamp albums. I've been teaching him about—"

Mrs. Lawrence cut him off. "Dad, I've packed those albums away, and they are not to be touched. Judge Brewster says you are not allowed to give anything away until he makes a final decision."

"Not allowed to give anything away!" Gramps roared, sitting bolt upright. "What do you mean? It's my property, isn't it? And what does Miles Brewster have to do with it?"

"Now, Dad, calm down," Mrs. Lawrence soothed. "You mustn't let yourself get so excited. Perhaps I didn't express myself properly. Judge Brewster didn't precisely say you couldn't give anything away. But he *did* say I have to give written approval of any gifts you might make, because I've been appointed temporary conservator of your property."

Laurie expected another explosion of rage from the old man that might lead to a major heart attack. Glancing at Matt, she saw that he was fighting to control his own anger.

But to her amazement, instead of bellowing with fury, Gramps suddenly seemed to relax. He leaned back against his pillows and smiled sweetly at Mrs. Lawrence. Then he turned to Laurie. "Laurie, would you please hand me that pad of paper and the pen over there on the table? I'm sure my daughter will have no objection to this one little remembrance I want to give to Matthew."

Laurie brought the writing materials to Gramps, and they all watched curiously as he began jotting notes on the pad.

"There!" he said when he had finished, and signed his name with a flourish. "I don't think it will upset the good judge if I give this to Matthew, do you, Margaret?"

Mrs. Lawrence leaned over and peered at the paper suspiciously. "What on earth is this, Dad? It looks like a list of Bible verses."

Gramps nodded. "That's exactly what it is. Those verses contain some special thoughts I want to leave with Matthew. Now, will you please sign this to indicate your approval?" He thrust the pad into her hands.

"Dad, you're being silly!" Mrs. Lawrence said, clearly annoyed. "I don't have to approve something like this."

"Margaret, this is a gift from me to Matthew," Gramps said patiently. "If you have to approve my gifts, you might as well start with this one."

"Oh, all right—if you insist," she sighed. Taking the pen, she scribbled her signature at the bottom of the page. "There!" She tried to hand it back to her father, but Gramps shook his head.

"You have to date it," he said. "To be official, it needs a date."

"Honestly!" she muttered, adding the date. "I can't believe you're making fun of me when all I'm trying to do is protect your interests."

"I'm not making fun of you, dear. I'm perfectly serious," Gramps said, but Laurie could see that his eyes were twinkling. He seemed to be getting quite a kick out of teasing his daughter. "Now to make sure this will stand up in a court of law, we need an unbiased witness. Laurie, would you please ring for the nurse?"

"Dad, this is utterly ridiculous!" Mrs. Lawrence fumed. "I know you're opposed to my taking control of your property, but it's for your own good."

Gramps nodded and smiled. "Believe me, Margaret, I understand completely. Once Nurse Watkins witnesses this gift, everything will be legal and proper for you and Judge Brewster."

Nurse Watkins was not pleased to find her patient's room full of visitors. "You two will have to leave," she snapped, frowning at Laurie and Matt. "Mr. Allerton is not up to all this excitement."

"Now, Bessie, they'll be going in just a minute," Gramps assured her. "But first, we need your signature. My daughter and I have both signed this document, and we need an impartial witness."

She glanced at the paper he handed her, rolled her eyes, shrugged her shoulders, and scrawled her signature beneath his and Mrs. Lawrence's.

Gramps scanned the paper one last time, then heaved a satisfied sigh. "Matthew," he said gently, "these verses have a very special meaning. They were passed along to me by my grandmother, who received them from *her* mother, many, many years ago. I hope they will bring you blessings. They are my parting gift to you."

116

As Matt took the paper, he blinked back the tears that filled his eyes. "Thanks, Gramps," he said, leaning over to hug the old man. "You'll always be my best friend." Abruptly he turned away to conceal his emotion.

While Nurse Watkins waited impatiently and Mrs. Lawrence scowled, Laurie bent down and planted a kiss on Gramps's bearded cheek. "Good luck with your surgery, Mr. Allerton," she murmured around the lump in her throat. "We'll miss you."

He squeezed her hand but didn't speak until she and Matt were about to leave the room. Then he said suddenly, "Matthew, I don't think I ever told you that my great-grandmother was a missionary to Hawaii."

Both Laurie and Matt stopped in their tracks. They both turned to stare at the old man, and as Laurie watched, she saw a look of understanding pass between them. Gramps didn't say another word. He just slowly nodded his head. Neither Mrs. Lawrence nor the nurse seemed to notice the silent exchange, but Laurie felt as though an electric current were flowing between Matt and Gramps.

Matt grabbed Laurie's hand and quickly stepped into the hall, pulling her with him. As soon as the door closed behind them, Laurie whispered, "Matt, what did that mean? What was Gramps trying to tell you?"

He started walking so fast that Laurie almost had to run to keep up with him. "Wait till we're outside," he whispered back.

Instead of taking the elevator, they hurried down the stairs to the first floor. Matt returned their visitor's passes to the receptionist, wished her a polite "Good evening," and walked sedately through the main entrance.

The minute they were outside, Laurie stopped and tugged at Matt's arm. "Gramps didn't really mean that his great-grandmother was a Hawaiian missionary, did he?" she asked.

"No," Matt said, shaking his head. "I'm sure he meant that his gift to me has something to do with his stamp collection."

"But Mrs. Lawrence took all his albums," Laurie reminded him. "What does that paper say, anyway?"

Matt took the message out of his jacket pocket and began to read aloud. "I, William T. Allerton, hereby make this gift to Matthew Harding . . ."

"Go on," Laurie urged eagerly.

"There's the list of Bible verses, the signatures, and that's all," he said. "I don't know what those verses say, but I *do* know that Gramps is giving me some kind of message in our secret code. We've got to get a Bible right away and find out what that message is."

"Let's go to my house," Laurie suggested as they hurried down the hospital steps, hand in hand. "It's closer."

She was almost out of breath by the time they rounded the corner onto her street. "Do you think Mrs. Lawrence will make trouble for you if she finds out that Gramps left you a secret message?" she gasped. "I mean, what if it refers to something really valuable? Even though she signed the paper and Nurse Watkins witnessed it, I bet she could find some way around it if she tried. She could say Gramps wasn't of sound mind when he wrote it."

Matt slowed his pace a little and gave Laurie's hand a squeeze. "We'll worry about that after we figure out what the message says. Besides, Gramps has a mind like a steel trap. She'd have a pretty hard time proving that he's loony."

Laurie's parents were in the living room, watching television, when Laurie and Matt burst into the house. Although Laurie wanted to snatch the family Bible and start searching for the scripture verses immediately, she first had to introduce Matt to her mother and father and report on Gramps's condition.

"Dad, is it okay if Matt and I go into your study for a while?" she asked when the formalities were over. "We have some homework to do."

"Certainly," her father said with a smile, and turned his attention back to an episode of *Masterpiece Theatre*.

Laurie strolled casually to the bookshelf, took out the Bible, and beckoned Matt to follow her into the study. Closing the door behind him, he brought the paper over to Mr. Adams's desk, where Laurie had placed the Bible.

"What's the first verse?" she asked excitedly.

"Jeremiah, chapter twenty-nine, verse eleven," Matt told her.

Laurie flipped through the pages to the book of Jeremiah and quickly found the passage. " 'For I know the plans I have for you,' " she read aloud, " ' . . . plans to prosper you and not to harm you, plans to give you a hope and a future.' "

"I love that old man." Matt's voice was husky when he spoke.

"And he loves you, too," Laurie said. "He's trying to help you. What's the next one?"

"Isaiah, chapter forty-five, verse three."

Laurie's eyes widened when she scanned the words. "Matt, listen to this!" she exclaimed. "It says, 'I will give you treasures from dark vaults, hoarded in secret places.' Treasures in dark vaults! I guess today we'd call a vault a safe. Does Gramps have a safe in his house?"

Matt looked stunned. "I—I don't think so. I've been over every inch of that house at one time or another, and I've never seen one. Find the next one, Laurie—maybe it will help clear this up. Ezekiel, chapter eight, verse seven."

Laurie felt herself trembling as she searched the book of Ezekiel. Matt bent over the page when she found it, his head close to hers. She read, " 'Then he brought me to the entrance of the court, and I looked and found a hole in the wall.' "

121

"A hole in the wall?" Matt echoed. "In the entrance of the court? I don't get it. There isn't any hole anywhere that I know of. Let's try the next one—Proverbs, chapter twenty-five, verse eleven."

When Laurie found the verse, she sat staring at it in confusion. "Does this make any sense to you?" she asked. " 'Like apples of gold set in silver filigree is a word spoken in season.' "

Matt didn't answer. He just gazed at the words with a puzzled frown.

Suddenly Laurie caught her breath. "Matt, do you think Gramps is trying to tell you that the treasure hidden in the dark vaults is gold and silver?"

"I don't know what to think," he said slowly. Then his face brightened. "Wait a minute! Maybe he wants to tell us where to find the hole in the wall! There's an apple tree in that little walled courtyard near the back door . . . I wonder if there's a hole in it somewhere that I never noticed."

"Sometimes you don't see things unless you're actually looking for them," Laurie said hopefully. "What's the next verse?"

"Numbers, chapter fifty, verse three."

Laurie flipped the pages back to the book of Numbers, mumbling, "Chapter fifty—chapter fifty . . ." She stopped turning the pages, her excitement fading. "Matt, there isn't any chapter fifty. Gramps must have made a mistake."

Matt shook his head stubbornly. "He couldn't have. Gramps knows the Bible from start to finish. Try the next two verses—they're from the book of Numbers, too. Chapter forty-five, verse two, and chapter forty, verse one."

This time Laurie didn't even have to look at the book. "There's no chapter forty, or forty-five, either, Matt," she said quietly. "The last chapter in Numbers is thirty-six."

"But those verses have to mean something," Matt insisted. "Gramps knew exactly what he was doing."

Laurie didn't want to argue with him, but she also didn't have Matt's faith in Gramps's memory. Her own grandmother was always complaining about forgetting things, and she was only seventy-three, while Gramps was eighty-three. Maybe his mind wasn't so sharp as Matt thought it was.

"There's one more verse," Matt said. "It's

Isaiah again, chapter thirty, verse twenty-one."

Turning back to the book of Isaiah, Laurie tried not to let her doubt and discouragement show in her voice as she read, " 'This is the way, walk in it, when you turn to the right or when you turn to the left.' " The passage didn't have any connection with gold and silver or vaults or holes in the wall. In fact, it didn't seem to make any sense at all.

But Matt wasn't discouraged in the least. "I know I'll be able to figure out what all this means if we can just look around Gramps's house!" He began to pace up and down. "What time is it?"

Glancing at the clock on the desk, Laurie said, "It's after nine."

"Do you think it's too late to go out there now?" Matt asked eagerly.

"I'm afraid it is," Laurie told him. "Besides, what if Mrs. Lawrence is spending the night at the house? If she found you prowling around in the dark, she'd probably have you arrested."

"I guess you're right," Matt agreed reluctantly. "She's actually staying at the Chilton Hotel, but she might have asked the cops to keep an eye on the place overnight. Then what about tomorrow morning? We could bike out real early—maybe six o'clock, before school."

Even though Laurie's enthusiasm had waned considerably, she couldn't bear to let Matt down. "Okay, but I'll probably be walking in my sleep at that hour," she warned. "I still have to study for an algebra test before I go to bed."

"Thanks, Laurie," he said, smiling warmly at her as she walked him to the front door. "You're a real friend. I'll meet you at the village green at six. We're going to find that hole in the wall, and when we do, all the rest of the stuff will fall into place."

"I sure hope so," Laurie said.

But gazing after Matt as he walked briskly down the street, she couldn't help thinking that Gramps had made a mistake. She wasn't so sure finding that hole was possible, but she didn't want to be a wet blanket. Besides, in spite of her doubts, she was very intrigued with what had now become quite a mystery.

Chapter Nine

Laurie was bleary-eyed the next morning when she began pedaling her bike to the town green. It was a beautiful spring day, but there was still just enough of a nip in the air to jolt her awake by the time she arrived. She found Matt waiting for her, pacing circles around the Pilgrim Monument, and as soon as he saw her, he snatched up his bicycle and called, "Let's go!"

Matt raced toward Maple Lane as though demons were after him. Laurie managed to keep up with him, but she was out of breath by the time they reached the top of Gramps's driveway.

Matt leaped off his bike before it came to a stop. "We'll start in the courtyard," he told her, running around to the back of the house. Laurie dropped her bike and dashed after him.

She hadn't paid much attention to the little walled court when she and Matt had passed through it on their way to visit Gramps's menagerie on Sunday. Now she noticed the beds of freshly turned earth and the old apple tree whose branches were still bare. It made Laurie sad to think that Gramps would not be there to plant flowers in his garden or to see the blossoms on his apple tree.

"A hole in the wall in the entrance of the court," Matt mused aloud. Walking up the two broad steps that led to a narrow porch, he began studying the weathered shingles that surrounded the back door. "Well, I guess you could call this the entrance. Laurie, do you see a hole anywhere?"

They both surveyed every inch of the door and the wall around it, then peered at the porch, the steps, even the foundation of the house. But nothing looked unusual or mysterious, and they found no hole.

Matt sighed in frustration. "I can't figure out what he means! Maybe I'm just not smart enough to play this game Gramps made up."

"It's not just a game, Matt," Laurie reminded him. "It's his way of giving you something very important that Mrs. Lawrence can't take away. And you are, too, smart enough! Read the exact words again."

Matt pulled out the sheet of paper on which he had written all the Bible verses. " 'Then he brought me to the entrance of the court, and I looked and found a hole in the wall.' "

"Well, if the back door is the entrance to the court, then maybe the hole is *inside* the house," Laurie suggested.

"Or maybe the back door isn't the entrance he means," Matt said. "Maybe it's the opening in the wall around the garden that you go through to the rest of the property."

"Okay, let's check them out," Laurie said.

Matt frowned. "But what about the reference to apples? The apple tree is right here."

" 'Apples of gold set in silver filigree,' " Laurie mumbled, looking up into the branches of the tree. "I wonder what he meant by that? What's 'filigree,' anyway?"

"You got me," Matt said with another sigh.

"While I look inside the door, why don't you see if you can find a hole in the wall around the courtyard."

But Matt found nothing, and neither did Laurie. They knew they would have to give up the search for now, or they would be late for school, so Matt made his regular morning visit to the animals in the pens. While he fed them all and checked on the injured ones, Laurie filled their dishes with fresh water. Then they mounted their bikes and headed back to the center of town.

"I know we're missing something in those clues," Matt said as they rode along side by side. "Gramps wouldn't make them so hard that I couldn't understand them, or what would be the point?"

"We'll figure it out," Laurie assured him.

"We've got to think about it some more and go back there again," Matt said. "Do you have a job delivery today after school?"

Laurie nodded. "Yes, but I should be finished by four-thirty or five at the latest. I could meet you at Gramps's place then."

"Can't do it. I have to work at the store till seven. But maybe we can go there when I get off. I'll call you, okay?"

"Okay," Laurie agreed. "And I'll try to come up with some more ideas."

For the rest of the morning at school, even while she was struggling through her algebra test, Laurie thought and thought, but her mind was a total blank. The "silver filigree" kept nagging at her. Maybe they should have been concentrating on that instead of on the apples and the hole in the wall. Since Laurie didn't know what it was, she decided to find out as soon as possible.

Before English class began that afternoon, she borrowed the teacher's dictionary and quickly located the word *filigree*. It was defined as "ornamental work of fine wires, especially lacy jeweler's work."

Laurie searched her memory of her visits to Gramps Allerton's house, but she couldn't recall seeing anything in, on, or around it that fit the description. Could the silver filigree refer to a necklace or some other kind of jewelry that was hidden somewhere in the house? And if it was, would they ever find it?

When the class began, Laurie propped her aching head in her hands, trying to concentrate on what Ms. Piper was saying. Suddenly the teacher's words riveted her attention.

"Henrik Ibsen's plays were originally written in Norwegian, but several people have translated his works into English," Ms. Piper explained. "It's interesting to compare the translations. Sometimes you get a whole new meaning when you read a different translation . . ."

Laurie sat bolt upright, her headache forgotten. The Bible was originally written in Hebrew and Aramaic and Greek. Over the centuries, many people had translated it into English. *There must be dozens of different versions!* Laurie thought excitedly. *What if the source of the verses Gramps listed isn't the same translation as the one Matt and I used last night? Just a few words might make a whole lot of difference. Maybe Gramps's message does make sense, after all!*

Laurie could hardly wait to check her theory. She was sure she'd never survive until the school day was over, but the final bell rang at last.

"Where are you off to in such a rush?"

Jane asked plaintively as Laurie shot past her in the hall.

"Song-A-Gram," Laurie called over her shoulder, not slowing her pace. "Talk to you later!"

Although she was desperate to ask Matt which version of the Bible Gramps used when they played their game, first Laurie had to make her delivery—and the final twenty dollars she needed for Operation Save.

Dressed in a buckskin tunic and beaded moccasins, Laurie appeared on schedule at the sporting goods store on Main Street. After warbling Ms. Vincent's lyrics to "The Indian Love Call" to the honoree, one of the employees whose birthday it was, Laurie politely declined a piece of cake and raced out the door.

Five minutes later, she was hurrying into the grocery store where Matt worked. She found him in one of the aisles, stocking the shelves with canned goods.

His face lit up when he saw her. "Laurie!" he exclaimed. "What are you doing here? Did you think of something?"

She nodded eagerly. "Yes!" Lowering her voice to a whisper, she went on, "Something my English teacher said today made me realize that different translators find different meanings in the same foreign words. There are a lot of different translations of the Bible! Do you know which one Gramps has?"

Matt stared at her. "Oh, wow! Laurie, that's *brilliant*!" He frowned, thinking hard. "Gramps has a big old Bible with all the family history written in the front, going back for generations. I'm pretty sure it's the King James Version."

"And that's not the one we were looking at!" Laurie was so excited that the feather in her headband was quivering. "I know we have a copy somewhere, though. Do you have the verses with you? I'll look them up as soon as I get home."

Matt took the piece of paper out of his pocket and handed it to her. "Here you go. Call me and let me know what you find out, okay? Mr. Porter doesn't mind if I get personal calls as long as they're important."

"I will," Laurie promised. "I just have to return my costume to Ms. Vincent."

He smiled. "That's too bad. You make a pretty Indian."

And then, to Laurie's astonishment, he

leaned over and shyly kissed her cheek. Laurie was so thrilled that all she could do was stare at him, wide-eyed. She knew she was blushing, but there was nothing she could do about it. Besides, Matt was blushing, too.

"Well, guess I'd better get back to work," he mumbled, turning back to the cans.

"I'll call you," Laurie whispered. She floated down the aisle and out of the store on a rosy pink cloud that carried her half a block down the street before she realized she'd forgotten her bike.

"Mom, do we have a King James Bible anywhere?" Laurie asked as soon as she got home.

Mrs. Adams looked surprised. "A Bible?"

"Not just a Bible," Laurie said. "The King James Version. I'm doing some research, and I need that particular translation. We do have one, don't we?"

"I believe so, dear," her mother said. "Take a look in the bookcases in your father's study."

"Thanks, Mom!"

Laurie hurried to the study and soon found the Bible next to some of her father's law books. She sat down at the desk and took Matt's paper out of her pocket. "Proverbs, chapter twenty-five, verse eleven . . ." she murmured aloud, opening the volume and paging through it.

Laurie's heart beat faster when she found the text. The wording *was* different! Instead of "Like apples of gold set in silver filigree is a word spoken in season," the King James Version read "A word fitly spoken is like apples of gold in pictures of silver."

That didn't make any more sense to Laurie than the filigree one had, but perhaps it would to Matt. She looked up Porter's Grocery Store in the phone book and punched in the numbers. To her relief, Matt himself answered the phone.

"Matt, it's me, Laurie," she said. "Listen— does this mean anything to you?"

After she read the passage to him, there was such a long pause that Laurie thought the line had gone dead. Then suddenly she heard Matt catch his breath. "Laurie, I've got it!" he exclaimed. "There's a painting of yellow fruit—mostly apples and a few pears, I think—hanging in Gramps's front hall right next to the door! And it's in a silver frame!"

135

" 'Apples of gold in pictures of silver,' " Laurie whispered. "Oh, Matt, that *has* to be it! That must be what he meant!"

"Do you think you could go to the house with me when I get off work tonight?" Matt asked eagerly.

"I'm sure I can," Laurie replied, every bit as excited as he was. "I'll ask Dad if I can borrow the car. If there's a problem, I'll call you back, but if you don't hear from me, I'll pick you up in front of the store."

"Better bring a flashlight," Matt suggested. "Mrs. Lawrence might have had the electricity turned off."

"Good idea. See you at seven, I hope."

At supper that evening, Laurie was so nervous about asking her father about the car that she hardly touched her food. As her mother was serving the dessert, Laurie said, "None for me, thanks, Mom. I'm kind of in a hurry. Matt and I have to go out to Mr. Allerton's place for a little while tonight."

"To the Allerton place?" Mr. Adams said. "Why? What's going on?"

Laurie briefly considered making up a story about helping Matt feed the animals but decided against it. She had to be honest with her parents. Taking a deep breath, she said, "When we visited Mr. Allerton in the hospital, he gave Matt a note telling him where to find a special gift he wanted Matt to have."

"A note?" Her father was obviously puzzled. "Why didn't he just give Matt the gift, whatever it is?"

"Because he didn't have the chance. When Mr. Allerton's daughter took him to the doctor on Monday, he didn't know he wouldn't be coming home again," Laurie explained.

Her parents exchanged doubtful looks, and she crossed her fingers under the table as she continued. "Could I use the car, Dad? Matt doesn't have one, and we'll get there and back a lot quicker if I drive."

"Well . . ." Laurie's father looked at her mother again, and her mother nodded. "All right."

"Thanks, Dad," Laurie said with a sigh of relief. "I'm picking Matt up when he gets off work at seven. I won't be out late."

"But if nobody's at the house, how will you and Matt get in?" her mother asked.

"Gramps—I mean, Mr. Allerton—gave Matt a key a long time ago," Laurie told her. "He trusts Matt completely, and he cares about him very much."

And so do I, she admitted to herself. *But does he feel the same way about me?* Remembering Matt's kiss, she shivered a little.

Laurie had never known an hour to pass as slowly as the next one did. She found a flashlight and tucked it into her purse along with the paper on which she had written down the new versions of the Bible passages. Then she tried to focus on her English homework, but it might as well have been in Greek. All she could think about was Matt. If the painting in the silver frame was the key to Gramps's secret gift, perhaps they would find it tonight. And if the gift really *was* a treasure, maybe Matt would be able to go to college and veterinary school and still have enough left over to help support his family!

At twenty minutes of seven, Laurie couldn't stand it any longer. Even though she knew Matt wouldn't be ready yet, she put on her jacket, asked her father for the car keys, and left the house.

Laurie drove very carefully to the store and pulled into the parking lot. While she waited, she tried to make the time pass quickly by singing all of Eliza Doolittle's numbers from *My Fair Lady,* but it still seemed like years until Matt finally appeared.

"Hey, this is really cool, having my own chauffeur," he joked as he got in beside her and fastened his seat belt.

"You won't think it's so terrific if my driving is as shaky as my nerves," Laurie warned, putting the car in gear and pulling out onto the street.

"Tell me about it!" Matt agreed fervently.

They were both too nervous and excited to talk much on the way to the Allerton place. Finally, Laurie came to a stop in Gramps's driveway. Before she turned off the headlights, she saw that the old Model A was gone.

"Mrs. Lawrence must have had it towed away," Matt said, noticing the same thing.

They got out of the car and approached the front of the house, which looked dark and lonely in the dim light of a half-moon. Laurie held the flashlight while Matt unlocked the door, then followed him inside. He pressed a switch and light flooded the entrance hall.

"Well, at least the power is on," Matt said.

Laurie blinked in the sudden brightness. The hall was completely bare. Peering through the open doorway into the living room, she saw that it was empty, too. Mrs. Lawrence hadn't wasted any time having her father's beautiful antique furniture moved into storage.

"What if the painting's gone, too?" she asked anxiously.

Matt smiled and shook his head. "It's not." Putting his hands on Laurie's shoulders, he turned her to face the wall next to the front door.

Laurie stared at the oil painting in its silver frame. " 'Apples of gold in pictures of silver,' " she whispered.

"In the entrance to the court," Matt added. "Or the entrance to the house, anyway."

"But, Matt, why do you suppose Mrs. Lawrence left it here when she had everything else moved?" Laurie asked, puzzled.

"Good question." Releasing her, Matt walked over to the picture. "Maybe it's covering something she didn't want anybody—like the movers or me—to see."

He reached up and lifted the painting

140

down from its hook, and they both gasped. There on the wall was a black metal plate with a dial in the middle.

"A safe!" Matt exclaimed. "The dark vault, the hole in the wall—Gramps wanted me to find this safe!"

"But how do we open it?" Laurie asked. "We don't know the combination. If only he had been able to tell you the numbers . . ."

"The *numbers* . . ." Matt echoed. Suddenly he let out a whoop of triumph and threw his arms around her in a giant hug. "Laurie, he *did*! The Book of Numbers! Those references must be the combination to the safe. Did you bring the paper I gave you?"

"Yes—it's right here!" Laurie's fingers were trembling so much that she could hardly open her purse. Finding the paper, she held it out to Matt.

"Numbers fifty, verse three; forty-five, verse two; and forty, verse one," he muttered. "How do you think it works, Laurie?"

Looking down at the paper, she said, "The next passage is the second one from Isaiah. In the King James Version, it reads 'This is the way . . . when ye turn to the right hand, and when ye turn to the left.' That must mean you turn right to the first number, then left to the next, and so on!"

"Okay, let's try it."

Very carefully, Matt turned the dial right to fifty, left to three, right to forty-five, and on through the sequence. But when he tugged at the handle, nothing happened. After two more tries with the same result, his broad shoulders slumped. "It doesn't work, Laurie."

Laurie concentrated fiercely on the paper she still held in her hand. Fifty, three—forty-five, two—forty, one . . . Those were the numbers, all right. "Fifty, three . . . fifty, three . . ." she mumbled. Suddenly she had an inspiration. "Matt, try doing it another way! Turn the dial three times right to fifty, two times left to forty-five, and then right again to forty!"

With unsteady fingers, Matt followed her instructions. They both held their breath as he grasped the handle and pulled. This time the door swung open.

"The treasure, Matt!" Laurie gasped. "It's all yours!"

Chapter Ten

Laurie wasn't quite sure what kind of "treasure" she had expected, but when Matt reached inside the safe and pulled out a thin, yellowed envelope, her heart sank. "It's nothing but an old letter!" she cried.

But Matt was staring at the envelope, an expression of wonder on his face. "Laurie," he choked out, "this isn't just any old letter . . ."

When he didn't say anything else, Laurie asked, "What do you mean? What is it?"

He looked at her, his eyes shining. "I think it's from Gramps's great-grandmother. She really *was* a Hawaiian missionary! Some of the stamps on this envelope are Hawaiian Missionaries, and they're in perfect condition! The five-cent stamp might be worth as much as thirty thousand dollars"—Laurie's mouth fell open—"but the two-cent stamp— Laurie, I've seen a stamp like this in one of Gramps's catalogs. It's listed at *three hundred fifty thousand dollars!*"

Laurie felt as if she might faint. Clutching Matt's arm, she whispered, "Three hundred fifty thousand dollars?"

She gazed at the envelope in awe. The stamps looked so plain! There were no fancy pictures, just a pale blue background with the words "Hawaiian Postage" and the denomination printed on them. The letter was postmarked Honolulu.

"Oh, Matt!" Laurie breathed. "It really *is* a treasure!"

Suddenly the front door flew open, and a harsh voice ordered, "Don't move! You're under arrest."

Whirling around, Laurie and Matt saw Officer O'Hara of the Chilton Police Department marching into the hall. Right behind him was Margaret Lawrence, and she looked absolutely furious.

"I knew it!" she screeched. "I *knew* that boy was a thief!"

Laurie was too terrified to move or speak, but Matt kept his head. Stepping forward, he said quietly, "I never stole anything in my life, Mrs. Lawrence, and I'm not stealing anything now."

"Then what did you just take out of that safe?" the woman demanded.

Matt looked her straight in the eye. "I took a letter Mr. Allerton gave me."

"Hand it over, kid," the policeman said, but Matt shook his head, holding the envelope tightly in his hand.

"It's mine. Mr. Allerton wanted me to have it. He even gave me the combination to his safe."

Officer O'Hara glowered at him. "We'll see about that. I'm arresting you for trespassing and theft. You have the right to remain silent. You have the right . . ."

When he had finished reading Matt his rights, Laurie finally recovered her voice. "No, Officer! You're making a big mistake. Matt's telling the truth! He didn't steal that letter—"

The policeman cut her off. "We'll settle

that at the station. Now," he said to Matt, "are you going to come quietly, or do I have to put the cuffs on you?"

"And I'll just take that envelope," Mrs. Lawrence said, thrusting out her hand.

Matt backed away. "No!" he protested. "Officer O'Hara, it's mine!"

Looking from one to the other, the policeman hesitated, then said firmly, "You'd better give it to me, boy. It's evidence in this case."

Matt's anguished eyes met Laurie's for a moment. "I think you have to do it, Matt," she murmured.

Reluctantly he surrendered the envelope. "Please handle it carefully," he begged. "It's very old."

The officer tucked the letter into the inside pocket of his jacket. "Come along," he said.

As Officer O'Hara led Matt out of the house to the patrol car, Laurie followed. "What's going to happen to him?" she asked frantically. "Are you going to put Matt in jail?"

The policeman threw her a sympathetic look. "It's still pretty early. We'll try to find Judge Brewster and hold a magistrate's hearing tonight. Maybe we won't have to hold your boyfriend very long."

"Laurie," Matt said urgently before he got into the car, "call my folks and tell them what's happened." She quickly wrote down the number he gave her on the piece of paper with the Bible verses. "Tell them not to worry," he added with a strained smile. "Don't you worry either. Everything's going to be okay—I hope."

Fighting back tears of despair, Laurie watched helplessly as the patrol car disappeared down the drive, roof lights flashing.

Mrs. Lawrence had locked the house, and now she turned her wrath on Laurie. "You leave this property immediately, young lady," she snapped, "or I'll have you arrested as well!"

The woman stood there, hands on hips, glaring as Laurie stumbled to her car. *Matt needs a lawyer,* she thought desperately, sliding behind the wheel. *Dad! I've got to tell Dad!*

Laurie wanted to floor the accelerator and take off at top speed, but she forced herself to drive slowly and responsibly. *It's not right!* she thought. *It's not fair! Gramps knew those stamps would pay for Matt's education and take care of his family, too. The stamps be-*

long to Matt. They can't let Mrs. Lawrence take away his treasure!

Laurie managed to hold back her tears until she got home, but the minute she raced into the living room, she began to sob. Both her parents leaped to their feet. "Laurie, what's wrong?" her mother exclaimed, running over to her.

Her father put his arms around her. "Are you all right, honey? Did you have an accident with the car?"

"No, I'm fine—the car's fine. It's Matt! He's been arrested," Laurie cried. "Mrs. Lawrence accused him of trespassing and theft, and he needs a lawyer. Dad, you've got to come with me to the police station right away!"

Almost before the words were out of her mouth, Mr. Adams was heading for the hall closet to get his coat.

Turning to her mother, Laurie said, "Mom, would you please call Matt's parents?" She handed her the paper on which she had written Matt's number and was on her way out the door when she had a sudden thought.

"Dad, I'll be right there," Laurie called to her father. "There's something we might need."

Running back into the house, she headed for the study. A moment later she was getting into the car, the King James Bible clutched tightly in her arms.

On the way to the station, Mr. Adams fired questions at Laurie as though she were on the witness stand. In response, Laurie described the visit to the hospital when Gramps had presented Matt with the list of Bible verses, and how she and Matt had struggled to figure out their meaning.

"Does he have the original list with him?" her father asked. "The one with the signatures?"

"I—I don't know," Laurie said in dismay.

Mr. Adams frowned. "Let's just hope he does."

As they got out of the car in the parking lot behind the police station, Laurie saw only one other car aside from the police vehicles—a luxurious silver Cadillac. "I bet that belongs to Mrs. Lawrence," she told her father. "I don't know why she hates Matt so much. She came all the way back from Boston just to get him into trouble!"

Her father gave her a quick hug. "Chin up, honey. She hasn't proved anything yet."

They entered the station, and Laurie rushed up to the crusty old sergeant who was sitting at the front desk. "We've come to see Matt Harding," she told him breathlessly.

The sergeant frowned. "Well, this ain't visiting hours. You can see him at the magistrate's hearing—Judge Brewster's on his way down here right now."

Mr. Adams stepped forward. "Good evening, Sergeant Cochran. I'm Thomas Adams, Matt Harding's attorney, and this is my daughter Laurie. I have a right to speak with my client."

"Now, Mr. Adams," the sergeant said, "you know a juvenile don't need a lawyer for a hearing. All the judge is gonna do is—"

"Sergeant, you don't have to explain a hearing to me," Laurie's father interrupted. "Matt is entitled to have a lawyer with him, and I want to talk to him."

The officer shrugged. "Don't make no never mind to me." Pointing to a door behind him, he added, "The kid's in there."

Laurie hurried into the small, bare room, followed by her father. Matt was sitting at a table, his face buried in his hands. He

150

looked so dejected and lonely that Laurie felt as if her heart would break.

"Matt," she said softly, coming over to him, "I've brought my dad. He's a lawyer. He's going to help you."

He looked up, and the despair in his face turned to hope as he jumped to his feet. Matt put his arms around Laurie and held her close. "Thanks, Laurie," he said huskily. "I should have known I could count on you. Thank you, too, Mr. Adams," he added, letting her go and shaking her father's hand.

Then the three of them sat down in the straight-backed chairs around the table. "I guess Laurie's told you what this is all about, sir," Matt said to Mr. Adams. "No matter what Mrs. Lawrence says, I wasn't trespassing, and I wasn't stealing."

Mr. Adams nodded. "I believe you. Do you have that paper Mr. Allerton gave you? The original, not a copy."

Matt touched his pocket. "Right here," he said, and Laurie let out a sigh of relief.

"Good," her father said. "Now here's what's going to happen at the hearing. It's not like a trial. Judge Brewster won't let me say anything while he's asking you questions, so I'll only be able to offer you moral support. Just tell him the complete truth, no matter what he asks."

They were all startled by a knock at the door. Sergeant Cochran opened it and announced, "The judge is here. Come with me."

Holding the Bible in one hand and clutching Matt's arm with the other, Laurie followed her father and the policeman down the hall to a small courtroom. Judge Brewster was already on the bench, and Officer O'Hara was standing before him. The only other people there were Mrs. Lawrence and a distinguished-looking gray-haired man seated at a table on the far side of the room. Sergeant Cochran led Matt and Mr. Adams to another table down in front, while Laurie slipped into a seat directly behind them.

"All right," Judge Brewster boomed, "I understand there's a question here as to whether or not a crime has been committed. This hearing is to determine several things. First, is there a prima facie case against Matthew Harding?" He looked at Matt. "That means, is there any evidence that you actually broke the law. Do you understand?"

Matt nodded.

"Second, if there is a prima facie case, can the accused be released until a date is set for a trial in juvenile court?" To Matt, he explained, "In other words, if we let you go, will you be a danger to the community, or will you try to run away."

Matt nodded again. *A danger to the community?* Laurie thought incredulously. *How ridiculous! And Matt would never run away.*

"Third, should the accused be released without bond?" Turning to Matt, the judge said, "That means, if there is reason to believe you might run away, you will have to give money to the court. When you appear for trial, the money will be returned to you. Is that clear?"

As Matt nodded in agreement, Laurie clenched her hands tightly in her lap. He had hardly any money at all. If he had to post bond, Matt might be held in the detention center for weeks. What would happen to his family?

Then Laurie thought about the two-hundred-dollar check she had just mailed off to Operation Save. If she called Aunt Missy and said that she couldn't go to St. David, after all, maybe Laurie could get her registration fee

153

back. But would Matt be too proud to take her money?

"I repeat," Judge Brewster was saying, "this is not a trial. We are here tonight to find out whether a trial will be necessary. Officer O'Hara, approach the bench and tell me exactly what happened earlier this evening."

The policeman turned to face the judge. "Your Honor," he began, "at seven-fifteen, a call came into the station from a Mrs. Margaret Lawrence. She had accompanied her father, Mr. William Allerton, to a hospital in Boston for heart surgery but came back to Chilton today to take care of some legal matters and to check on his property. When she turned into the driveway of her father's home, she saw lights in the house. That's when she asked us to investigate.

"When I arrived at the Allerton residence, Mrs. Lawrence was waiting outside. I tried the front door and found it unlocked. Mrs. Lawrence and I entered and found that young man"—he pointed at Matt—"and that young woman"—he pointed at Laurie—"looking at something. They were standing in front of a wall safe that was hanging open, and there was a picture on the floor underneath it. Mrs. Lawrence told me later that the picture used to hang in front of the safe to hide it."

Laurie felt perspiration breaking out on her forehead as she realized how incriminating Officer O'Hara's story sounded.

"I asked the accused what he had taken out of the safe, and he said it was this letter." The policeman laid the envelope on the bench in front of Judge Brewster. "The accused said the letter was his. Mr. Allerton had given it to him. He said that he wasn't trespassing and that he hadn't stolen anything."

"You say the door was unlocked," the judge said. "Had it been forcibly opened?"

"Well—er—it didn't appear to be"—even from the back, Laurie thought Officer O'Hara looked uncomfortable—"but I didn't really have a chance to look at it closely."

Judge Brewster nodded. "I see. And what about the safe? Had it been forced open?"

"Uh—I didn't have a chance to check on that either, Your Honor, because I had to bring the prisoner in. But I'll go back out there tonight."

Picking up the envelope, Judge Brewster studied it for a moment. "You say this is all the young man took from the safe?"

The policeman nodded. "We searched the accused after we brought him to the station, Your Honor. All he had on him was a wallet containing two dollars, fifty-three cents in change in his pants pocket, a bunch of keys, and a piece of paper with some writing on it in the pocket of his shirt. No jewelry or other valuables."

"What about the young lady?" Laurie flinched as the judge fixed his sharp gaze on her. "Did you search her, too?"

"Oh, no, Your Honor," Officer O'Hara said virtuously. "Mrs. Lawrence didn't say anything about the girl. It was the *boy* she said was the thief."

Judge Brewster shook his head wearily. "You're excused for now, Officer. Matthew Harding, please approach the bench."

Laurie leaned forward, biting her lip as Matt got to his feet and moved to stand in front of the judge. If only she could be standing beside him! If only there were something she could do to help!

"Mr. Harding, you have stated that you

were not trespassing. How did you gain entry to Mr. Allerton's house?" the judge asked.

Matt held up a key ring, isolating one key. "He gave me this key a while ago, Your Honor," he said. "I've been working for Gramps—I mean, Mr. Allerton, for over a year now, doing odd jobs around the place, caring for the animals, yard work—things like that. When he knew he wouldn't be coming back home, he told Mrs. Lawrence to let me keep the key because he wanted me to keep an eye on things for him."

Judge Brewster flashed a glance at Mrs. Lawrence. "So Mr. Allerton's daughter *knew* you had this key?"

Matt nodded. "Yes, Your Honor."

"But at seven-fifteen this evening you weren't taking care of the animals or keeping an eye on Mr. Allerton's property," the judge pointed out. "You were opening his safe."

"Yes, I was," Matt said quietly. "When Laurie and I went to visit Mr. Allerton in Chilton Hospital, he said he had a gift for me, and he gave me a note telling me how to find the safe because it was hidden. The note also gave the combination, so I could open it."

Out of the corner of her eye, Laurie saw that Mrs. Lawrence was glaring at Matt. She looked as though she was about to say something, but her lawyer restrained her.

Judge Brewster picked up the envelope again. "And this is the gift Mr. Allerton wanted you to have, the gift that's so valuable that he kept it locked away in a secret safe?" he asked skeptically.

"Your Honor," Matt said, "Mr. Allerton is a stamp collector, and he's been teaching me about it. The stamps on that old envelope are *very* valuable. They're probably worth almost four hundred thousand dollars."

Mrs. Lawrence sprang to her feet. "You see?" she shouted triumphantly. "Grand larceny, that's what it is, Miles Brewster! You know perfectly well that my father wasn't allowed to give anything away without my permission!"

The judge reached for his gavel and banged it on the bench. "Order!" he snapped. "You'll have your chance to speak in a few minutes, Margaret. In the meantime, please refrain from interrupting."

Trembling with fury and frustration, Mrs. Lawrence plopped back down into her seat, and Judge Brewster turned back to Matt. "You say Mr. Allerton gave you a note telling you how to find this hidden safe and open it. Can you produce that note?"

Matt promptly pulled the crumpled piece of paper out of his pocket and handed it to the judge. Judge Brewster adjusted his glasses and scanned the note, then scowled at Matt. "Is this your idea of a joke, young man?" he roared. "This is nothing but a list of scripture references!"

"Dad!" Laurie blurted. When her father turned around, she thrust the Bible into his hands. Without a word, he carried it to the front of the room and laid it on the bench in front of the judge, then returned to his seat.

"Please look up the verses, Your Honor," Matt urged.

Still scowling, Judge Brewster began to page through the volume.

Chapter Eleven

The courtroom was completely silent except for the rustling of pages and a few mumbled words from the judge. Laurie heard him mutter, " 'Treasures of darkness' . . . 'door of the court' . . . 'hole in the wall' . . . Hmmm. Knowing the way the old fellow's mind works, I think I'm beginning to understand. 'Apples of gold in pictures of silver' . . ."

Frowning, Judge Brewster asked Matt suspiciously, "What's all this about gold and silver?"

"That's the painting, Your Honor," Matt told him, "the one that was hanging over the safe. It's a picture of yellow fruit in a silver frame."

The judge went back to his Bible study. A moment later he looked up again, shaking his head. "I thought Bill knew his scripture better than this. The Book of Numbers doesn't have these chapters."

"I know, sir," Matt said. "That stumped us, too, at first, but then Laurie figured out that Gramps was using those numbers to tell me the combination to the safe."

To Laurie's amazement, Judge Brewster threw back his head and laughed heartily. "The old rascal!" he said. "Nobody but Bill Allerton would think up a code like this! You may sit down, Mr. Harding. Margaret, now it's your turn."

As Mrs. Lawrence marched to the front of the room and Matt returned to his seat, he smiled tentatively at Laurie and she smiled back. But she couldn't help feeling nervous about what Gramps's daughter would have to say.

"Well, Margaret," the judge said, "it seems clear to me that your father intended Matt Harding to have these stamps. I find no evidence whatsoever of either trespassing or theft. Have you anything further to add?"

"I do indeed!" Mrs. Lawrence snapped. "You know perfectly well that my father is not mentally competent to handle his own affairs. He gave money away as if it were scrap paper! Why, just before I arrived on Monday morning, he mailed off a check for eight hundred dollars to some organization called Operation Save." She spun around and pointed at Laurie. "Apparently that Adams girl talked him into it. She and the Harding boy make a fine pair, I must say!"

Laurie felt tears of gratitude welling up in her eyes. Ill though he was, Gramps had remembered her project.

"May I remind you, Judge Brewster," Mrs. Lawrence went on, "that I have a court order, signed by *you* on Monday afternoon, naming me a temporary conservator of Dad's property. According to the terms of that order, he can't give away anything more without my express written consent."

The judge nodded. "I remember perfectly well." Picking up Gramps's note, he held it out for her inspection. "Is this or is this not your signature?"

Mrs. Lawrence barely glanced at it. "Yes, it is, but I only signed it to humor the poor dotty old man."

"And when did your father write this note?" Judge Brewster inquired mildly.

"In the hospital room when Matthew and that girl came to see him."

"And you were there while he was writing it?"

She nodded. "I certainly was. I wasn't about to leave him alone with two greedy teenagers!"

Furious, it was all Laurie could do to prevent herself from shouting "We're not greedy! *You're* the greedy one!"

"It must have taken him a very long time to look through the Bible and find all the right verses to communicate his message," the judge said. "Didn't you suspect he was up to something?"

"He didn't look them up," Mrs. Lawrence snapped. "He wrote them from memory."

A broad smile spread over the judge's face. "'He wrote them from memory,'" he repeated, "and yet you consider him mentally incompetent. I only wish my mind were that sharp!" The smile faded. "Mrs. Lawrence," he

163

said formally, "the evidence presented here does not support any charges whatsoever against Matthew Harding. Your father obviously thinks very highly of this young man and wanted to give him a valuable gift. Despite your known opposition, he cleverly managed to gain both your written approval and the signature of a valid witness. Now, please go back to Boston and see him safely through his surgery like the loving daughter he deserves. And by the way, give Bill my best." He banged his gavel once again. "Case dismissed."

Mrs. Lawrence seemed to shrivel like a balloon that had just been pricked with a pin. As she turned away in defeat, Judge Brewster got down from the bench and walked over to Matt, the precious envelope in his hand.

"Matt," he said warmly, "you probably don't know that Mr. Allerton spoke of you often. He once told me you wanted to go to college and become a veterinarian." Giving the envelope to Matt, he went on, "You make him proud of you, understand?"

Matt could barely speak. "I'll do my best, sir," he promised, shaking the judge's hand.

Laurie wanted to shout for joy, but somehow she managed to control herself while her father took the Bible from the bench and the three of them left the police station. Once they were in the parking lot, she threw her arms around Matt. "Oh, Matt, I'm so happy for you! It's almost too good to be true!"

"I know. I can't quite believe it yet," he said, hugging her tightly. Gazing into her eyes, he whispered, "Thanks for everything, Laurie. Without you, I might never have figured out Gramps's message."

Mr. Adams smiled at them. "Come on, you two," he said as he got into the car. "Let's go home so Matt can call his parents and tell them the good news."

On the way to Laurie's house, her father added, "Matt, there's a safe in my office. Why don't you put your 'treasure' there for the time being? Then when you're ready to sell the stamps, I'd be happy to help you locate a reputable dealer."

Matt nodded gratefully. "Thanks, Mr. Adams. I'll take you up on that."

As soon as they entered the house, Matt phoned his parents while Laurie and her father began to tell her mother what had happened. When Matt joined them in the living room, he finished the story. Mrs. Adams was as thrilled as the rest of them were by its happy outcome and insisted that a celebration was in order. She and Laurie brought a pitcher of milk and the chocolate cake left over from dessert into the dining room, and they all sat down at the table. But before they dug into the cake, Matt raised his glass.

"I'd like to propose a toast," he said softly. "To Gramps Allerton, who has given me a hope and a future."

Only Laurie recognized his reference to the first of the verses in Gramps's message. Her eyes met Matt's, and as they drank the toast, they exchanged a smile of tender understanding.

Suddenly Mrs. Adams touched her forehead, as though turning on her memory. "Oh, Laurie, I completely forgot! Jane's been trying to reach you all evening. She was phoning every fifteen minutes, and she finally said you were to call her as soon as you came home, no matter what time it was."

Puzzled, Laurie said, "I wonder what she

wants. I guess I'd better give her a call and find out what's up."

Though she hated to leave Matt's side, she hurried into the hall and dialed Jane's number. Her friend picked up in the middle of the first ring.

"Laurie!" she squealed. "Where have you been? Your mom was very mysterious on the phone." Before Laurie could reply, Jane said, "Never mind—I've got the most fantastic news! Wait till you hear!"

Laurie laughed. "I've got some pretty fantastic news, too, but you go first."

"You're not going to *believe* this," Jane burbled, "but Elaine Desmond has dropped out of the show!"

"You're *kidding*!" Laurie gasped. "What happened? Is she sick? Was she in an accident?"

"None of the above. Her aunt invited Elaine to visit her in Paris for a month, and she's leaving next week! She says it's the chance of a lifetime, and she wouldn't miss it for anything."

Laurie sputtered, "But—but how can she do that? Ms. O'Connor will have to cancel the show! How can she just walk out and leave the rest of you in the lurch after all your hard work?"

Jane snorted. "Come on, Laurie! Since when does Elaine care two cents for anyone else?"

"Wow!" Laurie breathed. "Ms. O'Connor must be going ballistic!"

"She was—until I told her you know all of Eliza Doolittle's songs *and* all the lines! She says if you'll take over the part, she'll schedule rehearsals around your job, rehearse at midnight—*anything*!"

Laurie was stunned. She held the receiver at arm's length and stared at it, unable to believe what she had just heard.

"Laurie? Say something! Are you still there?" Jane squawked, her voice sounding tinny and distant.

Returning the phone to her ear, Laurie choked, "Yes, I'm still here. But, Jane, it's only two weeks until the show opens!"

"I know that. You can learn the blocking in no time, I'm sure of it." Then she added craftily, "Besides, we *need* you, Laurie. You'll be doing a good deed for everybody involved. Say you'll do it, Laurie. Please?"

Laurie took a deep breath. She had never

been able to resist a call for help, as Jane very well knew. Besides, she was a born ham, and her acting juices were flowing again.

"Well—okay," she said at last. "I'll give it my best shot."

"Hooray!" Jane cheered, so loudly that Laurie's eardrum tingled. "I'm going to start calling everybody right now. Ms. O'Connor's going to be ecstatic! See you in the morning!"

Laurie hung up the phone in a daze, thinking that this had without a doubt been the most amazing, exciting, astonishing day of her entire life.

Matt echoed her thoughts a little later that evening after Laurie drove him home. Dr. Miller had returned their call and assured them that Gramps was on the mend. As they sat in the car in front of his house, he pulled her gently into his arms. "This has been the best day of my life, Laurie," he sighed. "Remember that song you sang at the rehearsal for Parents' Night?"

She nodded, snuggling contentedly against him. "Yes, I remember—'Something good is going to happen to you.' And it did, for both of us. It looks like all our dreams are going to come true."

"But you know something, Laurie?" Matt looked down at her, smiling tenderly. "The very best thing that ever happened to me is you."

Laurie shivered with delight. "Better than two Hawaiian Missionaries?" she teased.

Instead of answering, Matt pressed his lips to hers, and as they kissed, Laurie could hear her heart singing " 'Wouldn't it be loverly . . . !' "